Hog Butcher

Ronald L. Fair

Hog Butcher

Foreword by Cecil Brown

Northwestern University Press
Evanston, Illinois

Northwestern University Press
www.nupress.northwestern.edu

Printed in the United States of America

10   9   8   7   6   5   4   3   2   1

Library of Congress Cataloging-in-Publication Data

Fair, Ronald L., author.
    Hog butcher : a novel / Ronald L. Fair ; foreword by Cecil Brown.
        pages cm
    ISBN 978-0-8101-2988-7 (pbk. : alk. paper)
    I. Title.
    PS3556.A36H64 2014
    813.54—dc23

                                        2014007232

♾ The paper used in this publication meets the minimum requirements of
the American National Standard for Information Sciences—Permanence of Paper
for Printed Library Materials, ANSI Z39.48-1992.

For Guni Muschenheim and Marvin Young

Foreword

Cecil Brown

In 1966, the year *Hog Butcher* was published, America was in flames. The plot of the novel—about a young black man killed by the police in an urban ghetto—seemed to have been taken from the headlines across the country. Today, we have the Oscar Grant incident in Oakland and the Trayvon Martin incident in Florida.

In 1966, I was well aware of the police murdering black men. I knew about the Harlem Riot of 1943 that took place when a white New York policeman shot a black GI. I remembered the Harlem Riot in 1964. A white lieutenant, Thomas Gilligan, shot a 15-year-old African American in front of witnesses that included his close friends. The incident caused a riot of three hundred young people. Before it was over, four thousand people had rioted against the New York police. The riot started other riots in nearly all the major cities that year. In 1965, blacks in Watts rioted. For six days, Los Angeles burned; thirty-four were killed, a thousand injured, and more than three thousand arrested.

So when *Hog Butcher* was published, it entered a long dialogue about violence in the city. I was a graduate student then at the University of Chicago, and a member of a black literary group run by Hoyt Fuller, a tireless promoter of black writers. He invited Ronald Fair to give a talk to our group. I don't remember his actually addressing our group, but I do remember meeting him in a café with a few other people.

Mr. Fair was very determined regarding his life in America. Born in 1932, he had been raised by hard-working people. He explained to us that he had been educated in a school of stenography and earned his living as a court reporter. Despite the success of his novel, he talked about leaving America and becoming an expatriate in Europe.

With the examples of Richard Wright, James Baldwin, and Chester Himes, it was clearly possible to be a successful writer abroad—though *Hog Butcher* and *Many Thousand Gone* (1965) are still Mr. Fair's most brilliant achievements. *Hog Butcher* continued the tradition of protest fiction that was started by Wright and carried on by Baldwin, Ralph Ellison, and Himes. Like these writers, Mr. Fair looked at the violence against African Americans through the prism of art.

Mr. Fair presented a new style of writing in *Hog Butcher.* The story is told not in a traditional narrative mode, but in an impressionistic style that relies heavily on interior monologue. The style enables Mr. Fair to move into and out of the minds of different characters and back and forth between past and present. Along with Richard Wright's first novel, *Lawd Today!* (published posthumously in 1963), *Hog Butcher* can be seen as a milestone in the use of interior monologue to portray the consciousness of African American characters—a development that takes on more resonance in the context of slaves being forbidden from learning to read and write. Offering readers access to the minds of African American characters was an act of liberation.

Mr. Fair's narrative turns on whether Wilford, a ten-year-old boy who witnessed the killing, will tell the truth in court about what he saw. The only evidence is the testimony of those who were present. Events similar to those depicted in the novel continue to appear in the headlines, though in some ways times have changed. For many people, the Rodney King case was a revelation, altering their ideas about race relations and police brutality. The case also underscored the power of the camera as an eyewitness. In the Oscar Grant case, a policeman was charged and went to jail, convicted on evidence supplied by a cell phone video. Before the advent of video, the case in Hog Butcher is decided by the choice Wilford must make between playing it safe and lying or honoring his conscience.

Cornbread, Earl, and Me, a film based on *Hog Butcher,* was released in 1975. The reception of the film was very positive, mainly because black people were starving for representation in the cinema. It starred Laurence Fishburne as Wilford and Rosalind Cash as his mother; it showcased the work of young black actors who would become major stars, such as Bernie Casey.

The screenwriter had never written a script before and has not written one in the forty years since. White screenwriters dominated movies about African Americans then and still do. The director had a pedestrian take on the novel, just as the screenwriter did. What emerges is the brilliant work of young African American actors. It took ten years to bring the novel to the screen. Apparently, Mr. Fair wrote two drafts of the screenplay, but they were rejected by the producers. The project was sold two times. It is instructive to compare the film to *Fruitvale Station* (2013), which took only a year and a half for the young black director, Ryan Coogler, to write, direct, and bring to the screen.

That summer, back in 1966, I asked Mr. Fair when he intended to leave for Europe and become an expatriate.

He said, "Now!" He seemed to mean he would go at the end of our meeting, though it was some years later before he actually did. I got a telephone number where he would be in Europe and tried to contact him in Switzerland, without success. Mr. Fair has said that America rejected its black writers. Today, he lives in Finland and is a sculptor.

January 15, 2014

Hog Butcher

Part One

■

"You see that shot? Man, you see that *shot?*" Earl said, throwing both hands into the air and then hunching his back as the handful of pebbles he had forgotten showered down on him.

Wilford slapped his thigh nervously. "Sure I saw it," he said. "Ain't I told you already he was gonna do that jump shot? And with both hands, too. A two-handed jump shot! And can't nobody *stop* it, either."

"Yeah. Yeah. I know. I know. You been sayin' he was gonna do it all day. But they been playin' since real early—I mean *real* early this mornin' and that's the first time he done it yet. So you ain't so right after all."

Wilford frowned. "Earl, why you always gotta win? I said he was gonna do it and he did. That makes me right. Don't make no difference how long it takes him to do it, just that he does. And if that don't make me right this time, then that means ain't nobody ever gonna be right but you. This time I'm right. He did it just like I said he was. And that makes *me* right. *Me. Me. Me.*"

"Well . . ." Earl scooped up another handful of pebbles and piled them between him and his playmate. He leaned back heavily (for a ten-year-old) against the cyclone fence that extended around the playground. He turned away from the basketball game, studying the structure his hand was molding. He moved the pebbles into a cone shape; then, deciding there was too much dirt mixed with them, he leaned over and blew a cloud of dust in Wilford's direction, cleaning out his pyramid. Wilford never noticed the dust.

They were under a steady cloud of dust as the older boys ran around in circles under the single basket. After one side scored, the other would throw the ball into play from under the basket, but it had to be taken a reasonable distance from the backboard before players could begin to move in for a shot. For Earl and Wilford, who had never seen a regulation basketball court, this maneuver seemed to be a great waste of time; they were in complete agreement about the foolishness of the rule.

It wasn't often that they agreed, but fortunately they felt that good friends didn't have to agree. All summer long they had argued about pitching horseshoes and softball and swimming, and about the temperature and the rain and the snow last winter, and about who was the better ice skater and who had more girl friends and who could shoot the higher and longer stream of urine, and about who had the better grade of hair, longer stride, lighter or darker color, smaller feet, keener eyesight, and about looks, weight, school, football, track, baseball, pool, reefers, and wine, and always about Joyce Lester.

Wilford, even now, was angry when he thought about Joyce. It was all Earl's fault. It was Earl who had dared him to throw the bottle of ink on her. He couldn't possibly let the dare go, even if he did like her, and even if he knew Earl liked her too, and even if Joyce had smiled at him almost every day the last few weeks of school and told another girl that she liked him. Joyce was like a fragile bronze doll to him, neat and delicate, and although he could never let it be known by any of his friends, every time he tugged at one of her braids he was secretly examining and swooning over the texture of her fine curly hair. He had often thought about her, even when she was nowhere near, and smiled at the memory of her delicate face

4

and ladylike ways. "Boy," he had once confessed to the wind as he walked away from her, "she sure don't act like she's no ten years old. Acts like she's at least twelve, but, whew! sure glad she don't look *that* old."

And then he had often thought how she would change when she became *that* old and went through those times when she would be irritable and not want to run the way she did now and say she was too old for such children's games. He was thinking that when he threw the ink on her. He was thinking: Yeah, you get to be twelve or thirteen or like that and you'll stop speakin' to me and start foolin' with them older boys, won't you? Sure you will. Then he hesitated, but only for an instant. He knew his responsibility to his friend. He *had* to throw the ink on her. When she ran home crying, smearing the blue-black stain over her white dress as she blindly tried to wipe it away, Wilford was crushed. But he pretended it had no effect on him and handed the half-empty bottle back to Earl and they laughed about it. He knew Earl had tricked him into doing what he himself had wanted to do and he was angry. He couldn't figure out how Earl always got him to do things like that for him.

But this summer Wilford was learning how to get even with Earl. He was learning to talk just as good as Earl—to talk louder and longer and have his say. He could swim faster and he could shoot the basketball farther and though he couldn't beat him at horseshoes, he was bigger by a half a head this year and Earl no longer picked fights with him.

"I bet he don't shoot it again," said Earl.

"I bet he does," Wilford answered snappily.

"Okay. . . . Well, I bet he don't."

"And I bet he does," Wilford said, throwing his head to the side.

"Yeah, you always bet wrong. I bet he don't, and I bet I'm right."

"I don't always bet wrong!"

"Yes you do. You couldn't be right if I told you how to be."

"Well, I'm right this time. It's a bet now."

"Okay."

"Okay. You got a bet."

"I sure have," Earl said, flattening the pebbles gently, making a foundation for those he would pile on top.

They stared at the big boys. The players were stripped to the waist and their shirts were hung on the fence. The dust settled in their hair and on their pants and on their wet bodies, and lines of perspiration cut through the dust only to be covered by more dust. And although each of the boys playing basketball was normally a different color, after four hours on the court they had all become the same reddish brown.

It was August now and the pebbles that had been dumped at the basketball site at the beginning of summer to fill the depression the shuffling feet had cut were all moved to the side or forced into the ground and the dust had become as bad as it was every year at this time.

Under the backboard, where they received a great portion of the dust, were more older boys who waited for the game to end so they could play the winning team. This was the only significant audience to the players; the kibitzers who laughed when someone missed an easy shot and shouted in high-pitched voices when one of the boys refused to show enough aggression, or ran onto the court stopping the game when girls worth looking at passed through the playground with exaggerated movements of their hips. They stood under the basket and occasionally leaned against the fence and smoked and drank the pop the littler boys were sent to buy for the reward of a rubbed head and a promise that they would some day be allowed to play. They were all similarly undressed, for coolness and for a show of whatever muscularity they possessed; their shirtsleeves were tied around their necks and the shirts hung loosely down over their backs, leaving their chests open to receive the occasional breeze that drifted across the playground stirring up even more dust.

Earl and Wilford had their shirts tied around their necks, too. In the fall (again, just like the bigger boys) they would sit in the same spot, only they would be wearing sweaters, and although they were shivering they would tie the sleeves of their sweaters around their waists and let the sweaters hang down over their rear ends.

"Hey. You know somethin', Wilford?" Earl said.

"No. What?"

"We sure lucky to have so many rocks to play with."

"No we ain't," Wilford said with an authority that should have warned Earl that he had his argument already figured out and would stop his friend's talking this time, too.

"Oh yes we are," Earl insisted. "I bet there's a lotta cats ain't got no rocks to play with like us."

"Says who?"

"Says me. I bet they ain't got no rocks like this in Mississippi."

"You crazy, man," Wilford said. "They ain't got nothin' *but* rocks in Mississippi."

"Yeah, but they ain't got 'em in *playgrounds*, I mean."

A look of defeat came over Wilford. He thought of the stories he had heard of the south, and particularly Mississippi. "The lynching state" he had heard it called, and he knew Earl was right again. He didn't mind that Earl was right this time, but he was suddenly troubled by something his mother's boy friend, Charlie, had said to him once before he got so drunk he passed out on the couch. "Where I come from, boy," Charlie had said, "a nigger ain't worth shit. Them white bastards soon kill you as look at you. And after I been here a while, I finds out Chicago ain't no too much better. They don't string you up, but they don't let you get nothin' they got, either." He had heard Charlie clearly, but at the time he hadn't understood what it meant. Now he understood. Now he knew that it was something as major as not having a playground.

And for a boy not to have a playground for horseshoes and basketball and baseball and to chase girls around in—because if you chased them in the playground you could chase them for a long time and pretend there was just too much space for you to catch them and that way they thought they could run fast and you could keep on enjoying the game—well, that was just cruel, that was the kind of thing you just knew only white people would do to be mean; keep you out of their playgrounds just because you were black.

"Yeah, you right," Wilford said sadly. "Everybody knows about Mississippi and Alabama and the rest of them places down there." He scooped up a handful of pebbles and began shaking them in his closed fist. "Wait a minute," he said, his face exploding into a smile. "The white boys got playgrounds, ain't they? Sure they have. I know they got playgrounds down there if we got 'em up here—even in that no-good Mississippi."

Earl shook his head violently. "My old man says it's so bad in Mississippi even the white boys ain't got nothin', 'cep' them rich ones. And there ain't no too many of them." He found a bright green pebble, smooth and well worn. "Here," he said, "look at that. Now tell me that ain't about the prettiest thing you ever saw."

"It ain't," Wilford said after a quick glance.

"It is too."

"No it ain't."

"I say it is."

"Yeah, and I say it ain't. It ain't nothin'. It ain't nothin' at all. It's a stupid rock and that's all. Just a rock."

"Okay, then, if it ain't pretty, why ain't it?"

" 'cause it ain't."

"Miss Carter said 'because' ain't no answer, Wilford, and you know it ain't."

"Well, it ain't pretty noways. Besides, before long Mr. Smith'll be floodin' the playground and all for skatin', and them little kids'll come out at recess and slide on the ice and kick rocks all over it and it won't be no good for skatin' until he floods it again."

"Oh, man, heck," Earl said. "He won't be doin' that for a long time; not until next winter."

"Yeah, but that rock's still gonna be on the ice."

"How you know it's gonna be this rock?"

" 'cause I just know!"

"Oh," Earl said, satisfied this time. Then after a pause, "But it don't *really* have to be this one, does it?"

Wilford smiled. He had done it again; twice in one day. That was a new record. "Yeah," he said confidently, "it's gonna be that one right there—that one right *there*."

Earl nodded in agreement and tossed the pebble out into the center of the basketball court so it could begin the cycle again.

They sat together in silence as the big boys neared the end of the game. Finally Earl said, "Cornbread ain't made another one of them shots yet."

Wilford sighed. "He will. I heard him say he's practicin' that jump shot for when he goes away to college down South."

"Ain't they got no colleges colored folks can go to in Chicago?"

"Sure they got 'em, Earl, but he's gonna play basketball."

"I know he's gonna play basketball! He's gonna play football, too, and run track, too. I know that, too, so you ain't so smart."

"Well if you know so much, then how come you always askin' me to figure everythin' out for you?"

"You! You can't figure nothin' for yourself. How you gonna figure for me?"

"Who says I can't figure— Hey, look!"

Their attention was drawn to Cornbread, who had dribbled around one man and then another and stopped with his back to the basket, as if he were playing on a full court and had just been passed the ball in the pivot spot by a guard. He faked a pass to his right, threw his head and shoulders quickly to the left, then sprang powerfully into the air and turned like a dancer and let go a high arching shot above the outstretched hands of the defender. "Two points," Cornbread said as the ball sank through the hoop.

Wilford and Earl sprang to their feet, jumping and shouting and slapping each other on the back as if they had just won the state championship. They watched Cornbread as the older boys crowded around him offering compliments, and they listened as he jokingly passed the miraculous shot off as luck.

"Look," Cornbread said. "If you were six eight you could do it, too."

"I am six eight," a younger boy said, "and I can't do it."

"Well, then you'll do it next season when you get some more experience. All it takes is practice if you got the talent, and man, you got the talent."

They were warmed by his words; he was their inspiration, their god who never disappointed them, and if they had thought it manly they would have let go and cried with delight at being in his presence. Perhaps someday they would grow up to be as good as or even better than the giants they worshipped now, but that was a long time off and the present had to be devoted to storing up impressions of what they would ultimately try to be like.

The nickname, Cornbread, had been given to Nathaniel Hamilton long before he himself was ten, even before he could pronounce his real name clearly. Then he was a fat, round-faced, tobacco-brown toddler with no shoes and a stomach that hung over the top of his diaper. He was forever walking out of his first-floor apartment, turning around to slide down the front steps on his stomach, reaching the sidewalk, and bravely heading for the playground where the sound of children's voices beckoned him. And on these journeys, which at first terrified his mother but soon became routine enough not to disturb her, he always carried along in his tiny, pudgy hand a huge slice of cornbread to sustain him through whatever ordeals might confront him—a high curb or a puddle of water or a pesky dog.

The first few times he wandered into the playground one of the older boys or girls always took him back home, but soon the children, too, became used to his wandering and began to look forward to the smiling face, stuffed or being stuffed with cornbread. And when the boys saw him clear the gate and break into a run across the wide playground, laughing and kicking up dust as he ran, they would call out, "Hey, here comes Cornbread!"

But Cornbread had surprised everyone—especially his mother and father, who could not recall that anyone in their families had ever been more than five feet ten inches tall. He was just four inches under seven feet and weighed two hundred and twenty pounds. He played first base on the baseball team at school, ran the two-hundred-and-twenty-yard race and the four-hundred-and-forty, played end with the football squad and, of course, center on the basketball team. He was a fair student and managed to graduate from high school without too much extra tutoring.

He was offered twenty scholarships, all athletic, but instead of choosing one of the bigger universities, he decided to go along with a teammate to a Negro school in Washington, D.C., where he would be spared the burden of being a professional

11

Negro: always impressing whites, always waging the war of proving his worth, always living another life while away at school and at the same time longing to get back to his neighborhood where he was free enough to just be himself and be with people who weren't so confused by his presence. He felt that at a Negro school he would not have to be a practicing schizophrenic and might find that ideal environment in which he could play basketball and run track and maybe even get an education if he didn't flunk out while having so much fun. School was not that important. All he really wanted to do was play basketball, and to go on playing basketball after college until he was too old to continue. Then he would think about using the education he had gotten while having fun.

So in September he would leave for college and for what surely would prove to be the most successful career of anyone from the playground.

Earl sighed, just too full to take any more. "Let's get some water before they start another game."

"Okay," Wilford said, and they broke into a run, heading for the fountain near the field house.

"Hey!" Cornbread called out. "Where you little guys goin'?"

The boys slid to a stop, turned, and answered in unison. "Get some water."

"How about gettin' me a bottle of pop?"

"Yeah," they said happily.

"Great." He tossed them a quarter. "And split one between you."

"Yeah, that's great," Wilford said.

They broke into a run in the opposite direction. As they passed Cornbread he held out his long arms and stopped them. "Wait a minute. Wait a minute. That's no way to run." He drew a line in the dirt with his foot. "Now that's your startin' point," he said. "You seen us practice track, I know."

They nodded.

"Okay. Let's see you get your holes ready."

The boys each kicked two holes in the ground with their heels, beaming at being recognized and now coached by the master. They would perform well.

"That's pretty good," Cornbread said. "Now get down and get your toes in 'em and try 'em out."

They got down on their hands and knees and carefully placed the toes of their shoes in the little holes.

Some of the older boys began laughing softly.

Cornbread squatted next to the boys. "Now listen to me. The most important thing about runnin' the dash is gettin' outta the hole. If you gonna run track you might as well start learnin' how to do it now, understand?"

The smiles vanished as the boys grew tense and moved their feet around nervously.

"Now I'm gonna start you just like it was a real race and I want you to come outta there as fast as you can, run all the way to the store, and come back the same way—only don't spill my pop. Okay?" He stood up and backed away a few feet. The other boys formed a line behind him and looked on smilingly.

"Take your mark."

Their young muscles tightened and they stared ahead intently.

"Get set."

They raised their rear ends and leaned forward slightly on their shaky fingers.

"Pow!" he said.

And they darted off like two miniature, overweight trackmen. Earl was first away, but Wilford pulled up beside him within ten yards and they turned at the gate, left the playground, and raced along the sidewalk, snorting and pumping side by side down the long block, each determined not to let the other win.

The older boys laughed at the pudgy, undisciplined runners with their arms working uncontrollably, fighting against the speed they so much wanted.

As they neared the corner, both Wilford and Earl instinctively turned into the street and ran catercorner across the busy avenue, shortening the race. They reached the door of the store at the same time, four hands landing against the metal Pepsi-Cola sign that protected the glass, knocking it open with a noise and force that told Fred Jenkins he was about to be visited by some noisy, destructive, unruly little boys.

No sooner had they flung themselves against the counter than Wilford, gasping for breath, perspiration causing his face to shine like a polished pomegranate, blurted out, "Cornbread wants a Pepsi." He took a half-dozen breaths. "And he bought one for us, too."

Earl held his side and leaned over slightly, panting. He touched Wilford on the shoulder. "He don't drink Pepsi."

"Huh?" Wilford said.

"No Pepsi."

Wilford leaned against the counter, took one last tremendous breath, and then began breathing more evenly. "Earl, I'm gettin' what I told Mr. Fred—Pepsi."

Mr. Jenkins hadn't moved toward the icebox and his face, thin, wrinkled, almost white, and clean-shaven, hadn't altered the slightest from its usual bored-by-little-boys expression.

"No, Wilford, I know. I been watchin' him, man. I know he don't drink no Pepsi. You can't tell me I'm wrong about *that*. He drinks orange and grape and once in a while a Coke, but never no Pepsi."

Wilford looked at Earl reflectively. He could be right, he thought. He had just assumed that Cornbread drank Pepsi, but it would be terrible to be wrong. That would be like letting Cornbread down when he was depending on him. He looked at Earl closely and saw that Earl was now trying to raise himself up to his height, standing on his toes. Wilford was noticing for the first time how Earl raised himself up, although he now realized that Earl had been doing it since last fall, unable to adjust to the idea that Wilford had outgrown him. Poor Earl, Wilford thought, he's gotta be the biggest and the best at everything, no matter what it is. He noticed Earl's eyes, sparkling now, set far apart by a wide nose; dark brown eyes, almost the color of Earl's skin; eyes that were burning with intensity, flashing with the knowledge that he was right. Wilford looked closer at Earl's fat, round face, dark eyes, wide nose, and narrow lips, and decided that he probably was right. I better make sure, he thought. He wouldn't want to take the wrong bottle to Cornbread. But why did Earl have to say it? Why couldn't Mr. Fred say it, he said to himself. Earl's almost always right. But he could be wrong. Surely he could. He had been wrong all day so far and he could be just as wrong now. But something told Wilford that this time Earl was not wrong. He slapped his thigh. "What makes you so sure he don't drink Pepsi?" he demanded.

" 'cause I just know 'bout things. I know 'bout lotsa things you don't know nothin' 'bout."

The fury rose in Wilford. "You don't know nothin', Earl. You ain't known nothin' all day. If you know so much, prove he don't drink Pepsi."

"How'm I gonna *prove* it?" Earl said disgustedly.

"I don't know. But prove it or I ain't gonna listen to you."

"You better. You know I'm right."

"No you ain't."

"Yes I am."

Wilford gritted his teeth and sighed heavily through his wide nostrils. "All right. I know how you can prove it."

15

"How?"

"You run back to the playground and ask Cornbread what he wants.

"Okay," Earl said, taking a step toward the door. Then he paused, squinted his eyes, and stuck his finger in Wilford's face. "Oh no you don't. You think you gonna get me to go back for you. Oh, no. You go back."

"If you don't, I ain't gonna split the bottle with you."

"Yes you are."

"No I ain't."

"You better."

"Who says so?"

Mr. Jenkins slammed his hand down on the counter. "Gimme the money," he said dryly.

The boys looked at each other and seemed to agree for the first time that day. Wilford dropped the quarter on the counter and Mr. Jenkins slid it off the smooth top into an open drawer and replaced it with a penny change. "What would you boys do if I wasn't here to solve your problems?" he said, turning on the squeaky stool he spent most of his life riding, and stopping at the icebox door.

Wilford stuck his tongue out at Mr. Jenkins' back and Earl snickered.

When Mr. Jenkins swung back around he reached under the counter and popped the tops off both bottles and then placed them gently down on the counter, one (the orange) in front of Earl and the other (a Pepsi-Cola) in front of Wilford. "Now boys, you both like orange, right?"

They refused to answer.

"And you both like Pepsi. So you ask your Wilt Chamberlain which one he wants and then you split the other one, the one that's left."

They looked at each other and agreed, again, that Mr. Jenkins was not the kind of person they liked. None of the younger children liked him. He had a strange roughness about him that they knew wasn't cruelty but that still bordered on it. He just wasn't a nice person to them. And sometimes when they had a whole lot of money to spend and wanted to take their time and stretch it as far as they could—a penny for this and maybe two pennies for something else—he would walk away from them and tell them to call him when they had decided how much money they wanted to spend and what they wanted to spend it on. The little children had a unanimous dislike for him, but his was the only school store in the neighborhood and they had no choice. Besides, he had the best penny candy they had ever tasted.

The older boys got along with him much better. He even carried on conversations with some of them and advised them about school and finding jobs; and sometimes, when there were just boys around and no girls, he would tell them about being careful and treating the girls special, like ladies. And once in a while, when he was sure his wife could not hear him (if she was in the back of the store far away from hearing him), he would tell them stories about the war and the girls he had known in Italy and France and Belgium and Germany. He wasn't quite so old to them and they didn't think of him as a half-white, crazy old man. To them he was a friend and the older boys liked him and trusted him.

Wilford took the bottle of Pepsi-Cola and started out. "Cornbread likes Pepsi," he said.

Earl snatched the orange and beat him to the door. He opened it and blocked the doorway. "Wanna bet?" he said.

"Yeah, I bet you," Wilford said, pulling the door all the way open and running out before Earl.

"That ain't fair," Earl shouted.

"Ah, man, I ain't gonna leave you. Come on out. I'm waitin'."

Earl stuck his tongue out at Mr. Jenkins and slammed the door.

Wilford was waiting for him by the stop sign.

They stood on the curb, each waiting for the other to start. A squad car turned the corner and moved slowly toward them. They waited for it to pass. The driver looked over at them. "Hi, boys," he said.

"Hi!" they answered, waving frantically with their free hands.

The squad car continued down the block and they darted across the street, over the curb, onto the sidewalk, and ran as fast as they could, spilling pop all the way.

■

It was a rainy day. It was pouring rain, like waves passing over the entire city; one wave, and then a pause, and then another. It was raining when Wilford woke up, and raining when he took the garbage down the back stairs for his mother, and raining when he ran across the street with two pop bottles salvaged from the alley to get Earl to take him to the store and share the find. Earl took for*ever* to get ready, and it was still raining when they raced down the block in their shirt-sleeves and tennis shoes, dodging and jumping over and splashing through puddles. And raining harder still when they boomed against the Pepsi-Cola sign and into Mr. Jenkins' store, fully prepared to spend fifteen minutes to a half hour deciding what they would buy.

Ten minutes later they stood in front of the candy counter, their drying heads pinned against the glass display case. The bottles were standing on the soda fountain behind them where Wilford had boldly placed them when they entered, and Mr. Jenkins had yet to utter a sound or move from his stool. He was turned, however, looking out the window—at the rain, of course.

The door swung open. Cornbread ducked his head and entered, straightening to his full height when he was beyond the threshold. The boys were discussing the merits of one particular kind of penny candy with their endless, rambling no's, who says so, I says so, you don't know nothin', I say it's better, and didn't see him enter.

"Gimme an orange to drink here and one to go, Mr. Jenkins," he said straddling a stool.

He looked at the boys and laughed to himself at their customary but quiet argument. "Hey, little fullbacks. You guys gonna buy out the store?"

The boys recognized his voice, but kept their eyes on the candy. Wilford held up his hand and waved feebly. Earl turned his head slightly and smiled. Even Cornbread could not take them away from their candy.

"How much money you guys got?"

Wilford cleared his throat to get a deep-sounding voice. "Four cents," he said proudly. "I found two bottles when I was takin' the garbage down."

"Four cents!" Cornbread said. "Well, that's a pretty good-size amount. I'd say that's a pretty good haul for a day's work."

Wilford squeaked his head up and down.

"Tell you what," Cornbread said. "When it stops rainin', you guys come by my place and you can have this bottle, too."

The boys turned away from the counter and faced Cornbread in time to see him raise the bottle to his lips and drain it without stopping.

"Thanks, Cornbread," Wilford said. "Thanks a lot."

"Yeah," said Earl. "Thanks a lot."

"Forget it," Cornbread said. He wrapped his huge hand around the bottom of the remaining bottle and ducked out the door.

The boys rushed to the door to watch him run because he ran with such perfect form, his legs taking slow, even, powerful strides that moved him quite rapidly but always gave the impression that he was just coasting, loafing along. Mr. Jenkins went on looking at the rain.

Two policemen had answered a robbery call one block away

only minutes before. As they neared the designated address, they saw the burglar break into a run down the alley. They pursued him as fast as they could through the ancient alley (concrete worn away to the bricks of another day and bricks chipped and rotted to dirt and deep ruts and sometimes high mounds of garbage), hoping to catch him after they reached the street. The man ran out of the alley, past the school store, and ducked into a gangway between two tall buildings.

The squad car turned the corner, saw Cornbread running, and slid to a stop in front of the store.

Wilford saw a flash of lightning and heard a tremendous roar of thunder as the policemen jumped from the squad car and drew their revolvers. Then he heard four rapid explosions of man-made thunder and saw four flashes of angry, murderous lightning and Cornbread's body convulsing violently with each bullet that pried its way into his back before he crumbled, lifeless, heavily to the ground, the pop bottle flying into the air and smashing into hundreds of little pieces of glass that reflected no light at all on this gray day.

Wilford screamed, "Cornbread!" He flung the door open, knocking Earl into the soda fountain, and dashed out past the policemen, across the street, over the curb, up on the sidewalk, calling Cornbread's name and crying and running. He reached the body and slid on the wet sidewalk into the blood, thinned by the rain, and onto Cornbread. He raised his head and looked into two huge, lifeless eyes; eyes of a stranger, eyes of his dead, gone friend. He trembled as waves of sorrow passed over him and he felt a sudden loneliness he had never before experienced, a surging, pulsating anger and sadness and emptiness that shut out the rest of the world and sealed him alone, unprotected, and afraid in the nightmare adult reality he had just become a part of. He stared into Cornbread's eyes and watched the rain splash right into them. Then he shuddered, screamed, dropped the dead thing and sprang to his feet, reacting to the eyes that had now captured his consciousness, and ran, hypnotized, shouting in a voice that was almost not his own, "They killed Cornbread!" Shouting to the people of the neighborhood, "They killed Cornbread!" Screaming it to the world, "They killed Cornbread!" Preaching to his people, the black people, "They killed Cornbread!" Warning the white people, "They killed Cornbread! He wasn't doin' nothin'. He was just goin' home and they killed him! They killed him! They killed him!"

The police walked cautiously to the body, their heads pulsating, their minds cloudy from the excitement, each feeling a false pride to hide his shame, powerful and yet imprisoned by his weapon.

"They killed him," Wilford sobbed, running from building to building, waking the world. "They killed Cornbread!"

Suddenly people began responding to his call and appeared on the street and picked up Wilford's chant and said it to each other and shouted it to the policemen. Windows flew open and the message was called from window to window.

"They killed Cornbread."

"What for? He ain't never done nothin' to nobody."

"I don't know. They just killed him."

"That white mothafucka did it."

"I don't know."

"We ain't never had no trouble with the policemens 'round here. Why they gotta go and start some shit like this?"

" 'cause they ain't no damn good, that's why."

"They done killed that poor boy."

"They sho did."

"They killed Cornbread," Wilford shouted hysterically as he stumbled and fell into a puddle of water near the body, too exhausted to stand any longer.

"Get outta here before you get sick, kid," one of the policemen said.

Wilford looked up and saw a white face, drawn with tension. "You white *bastard*," he said.

"You better watch yourself, kid," the other officer said.

"Go to hell, you black nigger!"

The Negro officer flinched; he glanced at his partner and then back to Wilford, gritting his teeth.

"A peckerwood bastard and a whiteman's nigger," a woman shouted from the crowd standing by the body, many without the benefit of umbrellas.

They holstered their guns as if they had just realized they were still holding them.

"And that boy's just a kid, too," a voice shouted angrily. "Brave bastards come in here shootin' kids."

"Yeah, who the hell they think they are, anyway?"

A group of teen-age boys tore their way through the crowd, saw Cornbread, and broke into tears. They had to be restrained by the adults.

"We better get some help here fast," the Negro officer said nervously.

"Okay. I'll stay with the body," his partner answered.

"Check." The Negro officer ran to the car, pushing his way through the people filling the street.

"They better get that boy to a hospital," someone said.

"What for?" a voice answered. "As dead as he is ain't nothin' nobody at no hospital can do for him."

"They sure shot the shit outta him."

"They sure shot him all right."

"Always killin' somebody."

"Yeah, the bastards think they gods."

The Negro officer jumped into the squad car and called for assistance. He was about to get out again when a voice screamed from one of the tenement windows, "Murderers!" and a flower box crashed through the windshield, rocketing bits of glass into the policeman's face. He screamed, his eyelids shut tight, bleeding, pain radiating from them through his whole head. He staggered from the car pleading for someone to help him. And then more flowerpots, bricks, pictures, buckets, pieces of furniture began raining down on the squad car and into the street. Someone hit the Negro officer in the back of the head with a bat and before he slumped to the ground they were on him, beating him as if they had waited a lifetime to bring their vengeance upon the authorities.

The white officer had started to go to the aid of his partner when a teen-age boy broke loose from the restraining adults and punched him in the jaw, knocking him into a woman who clawed his face and kicked him as the crowd pulled him off his feet. And then they were all kicking him; they were fighting, screaming, crying, tearing one another's clothes to get to the policeman to feel his body give way to their pointed toes and cleated heels. The officer, grimacing with pain, blocking some of the blows with his hands and trying to roll away from others while at the same time covering his head, grabbed his holster, found no gun, and began screaming for help. His cry of defeat freed the crowd from any restraint that had been present, and each of them suddenly wanted to kill him. Women screamed uncontrollably and ripped at his flesh. Men and boys grunted and rammed their feet as far into him as they would go.

Sirens wailed in the distance—coming fast. People began running.

Wilford felt himself lifted into the air. It was like floating gently in a dream, and as in a dream he didn't care who was lifting him or where he was being carried. He was exhausted from crying, but the tears kept coming. He knew whoever was carrying him was running. Then he heard the sirens, too, and he realized there was danger. He was afraid of the sound they made. He was afraid of police. He was suddenly afraid of grownups—all grownups—now that he had seen what torture they could bring on a man, now that he had seen the butchers from the other side of the counter, black and white, carving each other to pieces. He was terrified.

He opened his eyes and saw that he was being taken up the stairs to his building; through the door, then up the first flight of stairs to the second-floor landing. He closed his eyes again but sensed that he was being taken into his apartment, and then he felt himself being placed gently, just as in a dream, in the big chair. He opened his eyes, looked up, and saw his mother's boy friend standing in front of him. "Charlie," he said between sobs, "they killed Cornbread."

"Yeah. I know," Charlie said. "Your mama and me heard you all the way down here. You saw it, huh?"

Wilford broke into waves of tears and managed to nod twice for Charlie's benefit.

His mother rushed in the back door, soaking wet. "Policemen's out there beatin' everybody in the head and kickin' 'em and cussin' somethin' awful. You find him?" she said anxiously, her voice preceding her into the living room.

"Yeah," Charlie said. "He's a little shook up though."

She saw Wilford and rushed to the chair. "Honey, what's wrong?" she said, taking his head into her arms.

"Cornbread was gonna give us his bottle, too," he mumbled into her bosom.

She looked down on her son with eyes that reflected a pain even greater than his; the torture of being a parent and knowing the child is in pain and not knowing how to stop the suffering. She looked up at her boy friend. "Charlie, what happened?" she pleaded.

"I'll tell you in a minute." He eased Wilford out of her arms and onto his feet. "Wilford," he said gently, "go take those wet clothes off, okay? And maybe if you lay down a minute or two you'll feel better, huh?"

Wilford nodded and began walking slowly. He heard the four pennies jingle. He ran his hand into his pocket and brought them out. He looked at the coins through cloudy eyes. "We was gonna buy some candy and Cornbread came in and said we could have his bottle, too, if we went by and got it and he left and they came up and killed him," he said almost to himself. "They shot him. They really killed him." He dropped the coins into his mother's lap and walked slowly into the bathroom.

■

It rained all night and Wilford slept and dreamed pleasant fantasies, his subconscious refusing to subject him to any further torture. The downpour brightened the leaves and cleaned out and plugged up the downspouts and made even the grittiest windows sparkle (on the outside, anyway) and lowered the temperature over the entire city and carried away into little holes, whirling out of sight, weeks of industrial grit from the thousands of factories throughout the city that breathed out their waste with pride as a symbol of power and wealth and progress for the people who hurried about under its protective covering.

By morning the sky was clear and the sun was at work drying the streets. The wind carried the scent of a beautiful day, clean, pure, like the beginning of a new world.

Wilford raised the shade and leaned out the living-room window, looking across the street to Earl's building. The shades were still drawn. Earl was not up. Then he looked down the block and saw a squad car patrolling slowly along the crosstown street. He watched the car pass out of view behind the tenements and he tried not to think anything; he tried to suppress the anger that flashed through his mind. He shut his eyes, resisting the urge to look in the opposite direction where it had all happened the day before; but his head turned, almost involuntarily, and he opened his eyes and was startled to find the street clean. He had expected to see something to remind him of the violence of the day before, but there was nothing. There wasn't even the usual dirt and broken glass. And for an instant he allowed himself the luxury of being a ten-year-old and said to himself: Maybe it didn't really happen. Maybe it was only a dream. Even the glass is gone, he thought. No broken glass! That was like not having any dust in the air or not having a piece of paper slap you in the face when you turned a corner.

"No broken glass," he said aloud.

He scratched his head and looked at the street in front of his building. Then he smiled. There it was, hundreds of pieces of glass, sparkling more than ever after the rain, but none up near the corner. This don't make no sense at all, he thought. There's always glass *everywhere*. He remembered running out of the school store only the year before and falling on the sidewalk, skinning both knees on the pavement and cutting his hands on the slivers of glass that were always present. They took him all the way to the County Hospital to have the glass removed; one hour on the bus and then two hours in the waiting room and finally a disagreeable nurse washed his hands roughly and then a foreign doctor, almost as brown as he was, came in, smiled, and began removing the slivers, all the while speaking with an accent like nothing Wilford had ever heard before. He had laughed at the doctor and when the doctor asked him why he was laughing he said, "I never heard a colored man talk as funny as you." The doctor had become alarmed, or at least it seemed that way to Wilford, because he began working more quickly with less care for the amount of pain he was inflicting.

The glass was gone for a very good reason. The glass, the pictures, the flowerpots, the bricks, the pieces of wood and the occasional shoe had all been swept up and carried away during the night. The sanitation department, on direct orders from the mayor's office, had been called out as soon as the riot was brought under control and erased every trace of the battle; the assumption being that it would be easier to maintain order if the people were not reminded of the cause of the disturbance. The authorities felt that by sweeping the streets and clearing away the debris left over from the fight they could make the people forget the shooting.

But what they didn't know was that many of the people in the neighborhood had never seen the sanitation department involved in actual work. They had seen them acting as if they were working, dragging out an hour's work to fill the eight-hour day—playing cards in the cab of the truck, sleeping by a fire hydrant, but not actually working as men worked, as the Negro men had to work every day to earn their week's pay. This most unusual event would be remembered for a long time: the day the city went to work.

Wilford turned from the window and sat on the sill looking back over the apartment. His gaze moved lazily across the linoleum and stopped at the small black mark from a cigarette his mother or Charlie had forgotten and allowed to fall from the ash tray that must have been on the arm of the chair—the one stuffed chair in the room that came from the Salvation Army store along with the matching couch.

It was Sunday and the house should have been cleaned the day before, but his mother had permitted him to sleep in her bed until late that night. Then Charlie had awakened him and told him that he must go to his own bed. He had gotten up and walked to the couch with his eyes closed and fallen asleep again as soon as he lay down. Charlie and his mother had made love with such enthusiasm that night that they woke up the people living underneath them, but not Wilford. He slept through the rhythmic creaking of the bed, the fallen bed slat, the knocked-over glass of whiskey, the thunder and lightning. He slept soundly and restfully, his sleep cushioned by the steady cadence of the rain.

Now he stretched, tilted his head to the side, and allowed his gaze to drift slowly from object to object without sending a definite impression to his mind. He saw and did not see the ancient wallpaper caked with oily dirt, and the dime-store print of the ocean with lavender water and reddish traces through the whitecaps, and the built-in china cabinet as old and worn as the building, and the rat holes that had been covered with wire mesh and then a thin layer of plaster and finally an unmatching wallpaper. He looked past the window sills covered with dust and decorated by rain drops, and then his eyes arrived at the couch and he realized he had lapsed into another one of his blank periods that he could never explain to his mother or his teachers. He couldn't explain the periods of void because he didn't quite know how to tell someone what it felt like to have his mind scurrying off wherever it wanted to go; his mind had yet to explain it to him. All he knew was that he always felt cleansed when he let his mind go where it wanted to go. He knew it couldn't be as bad as the adults said it was because he always felt rested, too.

But now he studied the couch with complete awareness of its presence and he remembered he had a job to do. He knew he would have to make it up before he could get away. It seemed that was all he did lately, make beds and scrub floors. Women's work, he thought. Everything around the house was women's work to him now that he was becoming a man. Washing the face and brushing the teeth and scrubbing the nails— all things women did, to be more like women. And his mother made him do them like maybe she thought he was a girl. Sure, he thought, as he folded the sheet carefully, trying to get the edges to line up (although they never would, not for him and not even for his mother or for anybody else's mother), she acts like I'm some silly girl. "Make sure you wash them *nasty* hands before you sit down to my table." "Look at those feet! How long you been wearin' them filthy socks? Well, take 'em off and get in that tub right this minute and don't come out 'til you got that dirt off you." "Don't 'ah mama' me, now. Just do as I tell you." "Oh, no, you ain't that black." "I ain't never seen no boy who bites his nails and still has fingers that dirty. Boy, you gonna poison yourself eatin' all that dirt."

I bet she wouldn't treat me that way if I had an old man. He'd help me out of it. A man ain't suppose' to smell like no woman, noways. And for a moment Wilford allowed himself to dream about the joy of having a father. Charlie was a nice guy and a real friend, but he was that way only sometimes. Often he appeared to be annoyed by Wilford. Still, he was better than no one. But a real father! Not Charlie. Maybe he was a sometime-father, but no real father. A real father was different. A real father wasn't always nice, either, but he was at least around and cared about you, he thought, and sometimes he would talk to you and maybe even laugh; and drunk or sober, at least he was a real father. That was better than a sometime-father. That was better than even a good friend like Charlie. He dismissed the thought.

He hadn't thought about having a father with as much seriousness in many years, not since he began growing up. Years before, oh, when he was five or six and the other children used to tease him and call him a bastard—that was when he would have given anything to have a father. He even went so far as to invent one. He told the children that Charlie was his father, but that he didn't live with them because he worked for some white people who made him live with them; and that his mother didn't want to live in the country, so Charlie (who made more money than anybody else in the neighborhood, of course, according to Wilford) had gotten their apartment so that his mother could live in the city and be happy, and Charlie, living on a rich estate in the country, miles and miles away, could only visit with them on his days off. Sometimes the other children saw Charlie leaving in the morning and if they felt particularly charitable, they pretended to believe Wilford.

But now Wilford preferred not to think about what it would be like to have a father because he knew he would never have one.

He placed the sheet neatly under the cushion, looked at his mother's bedroom door and then at the bathroom, and tried to think of something else to do to postpone the girl thing. He thought of how she'd look coming out of the bedroom in her cotton duster with the two bottom buttons still off after all these months, yawning and stretching; standing at the kitchen stove, striking a match, and lighting the burner under the coffeepot, her spindly legs seeming much too thin to support the robust torso above them.

Sarah Robinson was one of those unusual women who were overweight and yet delightfully attractive. She was even considered beautiful by some people. Her color was that of the leaves in the fall when all the picture-book fire is gone from them; her eyes were bright, her lips were full, and her nose was broad, the skin of her round face was still smooth and flawless, and she had a full head of hair that could be easily managed.

Sarah was twenty-five now and possessed a kind of angelic youthfulness. She had been fourteen when Wilford was conceived; an illegitimate child, supported by the county, reaching maturity at fourteen, and continuing the tradition she was born into. She had saved the state money by dropping out of school, but added another name to the county's swelling aid rolls. She turned fifteen the month before Wilford was born (eight pounds and six ounces), and she remained at home with her mother until three years later when she and Charlie got an apartment together.

In the beginning they had honestly wanted to get married, but Charlie earned only forty dollars a week as a stock boy and it made sense for her to stay on aid and for him to supplement the aid with whatever money he could spare. The problem with this arrangement was that they could not let Sarah's caseworker learn that Charlie was living there; the county frowned on its women having boy friends. Not that they expected them to stop being women and wanting and needing men (although there was that element that cried loudly for sterilization or cutting them off the rolls if they gave birth to two illegitimate children), but they simply refused to support the boy friends too. But Charlie was in love with Sarah, and when they found she had a difficult caseworker, they moved.

They moved often in the seven years that followed their strange union. The moving did not disturb them. It was not unusual to move two or three times in one year in a city where everyone was always moving. Not at all unusual to move often in a city that was constantly changing; in a city whose Negro neighborhoods were swelling, flexing their muscles, and breathing deeper into the municipal air the same way the city itself had erupted some fifty years before.

The last move two years ago, to the second-floor apartment across the street from the school, had been the most costly yet. Charlie was not living in the three rooms with Sarah and Wilford, but had taken a room with a family in the apartment across the hall. This was an unpleasant arrangement for Charlie, but Sarah had decided that she was tired of running from caseworkers who had no heart or understanding of the problems of her society. "Besides," she had said to Charlie to support her argument, "Wilford's almost as big as you already and he don't like seein' you livin' with me. And if he thinks we oughta live separate, then let's do it before he gets big enough to make too much of a fuss about it. I tried to explain to him why we can't get married, but he's too young to know 'bout things like this."

So, resentfully, Charlie acquiesced; sometimes he slept in his lonely bed in the strangers' apartment, but he still ate all of his meals with Sarah and Wilford. They remained together in this way that society and circumstances had forced upon them.

Like Charlie, Wilford now fell a victim to his mother's wishes, found his way into the bathroom, and began the thing he hated most, the girl's game, the foolish, absolutely absurd practice of washing his face even though it had been washed the night before and hadn't had so much as five minutes to get dirty again.

Gazing into the mirror he had no notion that he looked exactly like his mother. It was just as well that he was unaware of this resemblance. If he had known, he surely would have been embarrassed, and might have engaged in an unlimited number of fights until his smooth, girlish skin had been hardened and transfigured by the scars of manhood to make his masculinity obvious to all. He had noticed his mother's height, though, and this year the woman who at five feet one had towered over him for all of his life had finally begun to raise her eyes slightly when she looked at him. Sometimes he wondered how tall he would grow, but, having no father to compare himself with, he usually ended in frustration. Only, however, after he had tried to convince himself that he would surely be as tall as Cornbread, and much stronger, and perhaps just a bit more agile. He didn't want to be too much taller than Cornbread, just perhaps a hair, or maybe even a quarter of an inch, so he could play basketball with the best and lean farther than any first baseman had ever leaned to catch that wild throw from the third baseman that would result in the final out and win his team the championship.

He stuck his tongue out at the reflection, trying to provoke it to force him to smile. Then he remembered Cornbread and noticed the tears forming in his eyes. Seeing them gather, he blinked, and more came and overflowed down his cheeks as the flashes and explosions and blood whirled in his mind. Then the policemen came between his eyes and the mirror and dried up the tears and replaced the old expression of grief with one of hatred.

He went to the kitchen and poured a glass of milk. When he finished it he poured a second. Stuffing two pieces of stale bread into his mouth between swallows, he finished the second glass. The bread wasn't so dry that way. He went back into the front room, dressed, quietly unlocked the three locks, and sneaked out of the house.

Why'd they have to *kill* him, he said to himself as he looked over at Earl's window. He slapped his thigh twice. He wanted to talk to Earl about it, but he didn't want to argue and Earl would try to be smart and say he knew why Cornbread had been killed, even if he didn't know, and they would have another argument. "I don't wanna argue with you today," he said to the imaginary Earl standing in front of him. And for the first time in months he didn't go get Earl. He sat down on the steps and waited for time to pass, perhaps waiting for Earl to come to him.

Before long people began to appear on the street on their way to church. A man and his wife came toward Wilford from the direction of the store and he could see that the man's head was bandaged. A car started up and sped past. The driver's eye was swollen and discolored. For Wilford, it was like waking up one morning and finding that everyone had grown ugly. They weren't smiling and happy any more; they were passing in silence with fixed angry expressions on their scarred and tortured faces. Then he remembered vaguely what his mother had said when she came in and he realized that the police had probably spared very few people in their efforts to restore law and order. His fanciful mind told him the people had fought off the policemen in the district and reinforcements had to be called in. He decided that they could have won, but they didn't want to kill anybody (after all, they weren't like the police) and they had not fought as viciously as the police and in the end they were subdued by superior numbers who were better prepared for combat.

He heard a thunderous roar coming and looked up in time to see twelve officers, all over six feet, cruising slowly down the block on motorcycles. They were so big the motorcycles looked like children's toys under them. "The *task force,*" Wilford said as if answering the interrogations of his mind.

They were all white men and looked very tough and very mean. He had seen them earlier that summer when they passed through the neighborhood as they did from time to time to remind the residents that there was a special squad created not so much to protect them as to keep them in line. When Wilford had seen them earlier that year he was delighted and waved to them. Some of the officers had even smiled at him. It had been a thrill to see them, so well trained, like soldiers, their motorcycles passing two at a time, uniforms crisp and freshly pressed, shoes shined, riot guns fastened to the motorcycles and each man with at least two hand weapons. A perfect military machine—like police the world over; like the ones he had seen in a history book at school who wore black uniforms and, as his history book said (or at least he thought that's what it said), were the protectors of an old German government. But now he didn't feel like rejoicing about the parade. Parades didn't interest him today. Now he didn't wave. He sat on the step, a little frightened, and stared at them as angrily as they stared at everyone they saw.

After they passed he walked across the street to the playground to watch a group of younger children playing. The children were pursuing a series of spontaneous games with rules that altered as quickly as their movements.

First they chased the loose football, kicking it when they came upon it, like soccer; then, with no warning to someone watching the game, it was a delicate parcel that must be carried in one's arms protected from those who struggled to rip it from the firm grasp of the runner and begin kicking it again; then it was a volleyball and then a basketball to be tossed high in the air through an imaginary hoop; and then, alas, it became the kicking game again. And always the little children seemed to anticipate the rule changes and adapted readily to them.

At the other end of the playground, under the basket, just to the side of the pond where the basketball court used to be, the older boys crouched, a group of ten or twelve, talking quietly while the basketball lay near the fence behind them, rocking slightly in the wind.

Wilford approached the boys but stopped at a respectable distance and stood looking in their direction until he was noticed and called to join them.

"Say, man. You see 'em get Cornbread?" Chuck asked.

"Yeah," Wilford said, looking away from Chuck's cold, serious eyes at a group of pigeons who had left their nests in the attic of the school and were busily selecting specks of garbage and gravel from the alley.

He was jerked back into the conversation as Big Tommie spun him around to face him. "Where were you?"

"The store."

"Where was Bread?"

"He came in the store, too."

"Who shot him?" said Popcorn.

"Both of 'em."

"Yeah, but where," said Chuck, "in the *store?*"

"Outside."

Now Jesse spun him around. "Did you really see it?"

"Sure I did," Wilford said indignantly.

Little Tommie pulled him.

Sam demanded an answer to his more-pressing question.

Chuck encouraged him to tell what he had seen.

Wilford began talking, slowly at first, then picked up speed as he relived the experience step by step until he had finished and slumped against the fence, limp, almost as exhausted as the day before.

Horse grumbled angrily.

Stringbean rocked like a tall tree swaying in the wind.

Little Hippy grasped his forehead dramatically and poked his finger up and onto the chest of Al, demanding vengeance.

Mouse moved his lips nervously.

Fat produced—even for him—an unbelievable amount of perspiration and breathed heavily through his open mouth.

Wilford sighed, as if the weight had been lifted by his telling the story, and fell silent, proudly silent that they had listened to him with complete attention for all of three minutes.

"See that," Chuck said. "I told you them crackers was tryin' to start some shit. I knew damn well Bread wasn't breakin' into nobody's house. They just tryin' to cover up."

"Yeah," said Little Hippy. "But that's what the police believe. That's what they told his folks and all them people they rounded up yesterday."

"And I bet you believed it, too, didn't you?" said Chuck. "You dumb ass. You can't believe no white cat—*never*." Chuck gritted his teeth. "Some day, man . . . some day . . ." He sent two vicious blows into the midsection of an imaginary opponent, grunting to muster that little extra power. "Man, the time's comin' when we ain't gonna take no more of this shit."

"We gotta do *somethin'*," said Little Tommie.

Jesse, Horse, Mouse, Fat all joined in. "Yeah, yeah." "Damn right." "Like today!"

"Maybe we can," Chuck said, and he looked around the playground, searching the cyclone fence for an answer. "Maybe we can do somethin' to upset these ofays like they ain't never been upset. We been around here playin' basketball and football and all that jazz all this time when we shoulda been out kickin' some ass."

The roar of motorcycles was heard as the overweight forms bulging around, hanging over the air-cooled bikes, two by two, appeared on the block again, snarling contemptuously as they looked from side to side searching doorways, gangways, porches for someone willing to offer resistance so they could whip the neighborhood into shape and show how efficiently things could have been handled the day before if they had been summoned instead of the patrolmen from the local district. "They should 'f sent us in," the sergeant told his commander. "We would 'f had them niggers in line in less than fifteen minutes. But *two* hours to stop a bunch of black bastards —that's unheard of. That's what they get for not calling us in. Just let 'em start something while my boys are out there. Just let 'em!"

Horse said, "Here come the blue shirts."

Chuck put his hand on Wilford's head. "You better get outta here," he said in a fatherly way. "And don't tell the fuzz nothin'. Don't never tell a white man nothin' 'cause he'll just twist it to fit what he wants it to say. Now get outta here."

Wilford trotted to the middle of the playground, turned, and watched the hefty policemen curb their motorcycles, leaving the motors running, clanging like diesel engines. "Come here!" an authoritative voice bellowed out over the roar of the engines, over the screams of the smaller children excited by the motorcycles.

The older boys ignored him. They began passing the basketball among them.

The task-force men reacted quickly to this open defiance. Under normal conditions they might have given the boys at least one other chance to respond, but this was the riot area and they had orders not to let crowds form on the street. Two of the younger, less obese officers led the foot race, running right into the boys and knocking them against the fence.

"All right, you guys know the route. Turn around, spread your legs out and lean against the fence."

The boys refused to move.

"Oh," the officer said. "We got some tough guys here. Next thing I know someone'll ask for a search warrant."

Chuck faced the fence, spread his legs wide apart, and

leaned forward with his arms outstretched until his hands came to rest against the fence. The other boys followed his lead in silence.

"Now that's smart. Thought we were going to have to let you punks see the inside of the station. Might have to yet."

By now Wilford had worked his way out of the playground and was standing behind a parked car, looking through the windows as the boys were being searched. His heart was pounding so loudly he could hear it over the noise of the engines. His young eyes showed a kind of anger that should have been foreign to a ten-year-old, and his fingers slid over the glass as he tried mechanically to grip it. The police began pushing the boys around, slapping them and shouting insults at them, trying to provoke some form of resistance.

Wilford wanted to do something to help the older boys. Next to him in the street, shielded by the car, were the four lead motorcycles, their motors idling clumsily and loudly. He'd blow one of the horns. But that would only bring one officer to chase him away. He'd break their rear-view mirrors. Nothing to break them with. I gotta do *somethin'*, he said to himself. Then he noticed a key chain dangling from the ignition of one of the motorcycles. He checked the other three quickly and they also had fancy key chains, all seeming to sway uniformly as the machines vibrated. That's it! he thought. I'll get 'em now.

Realizing that he was about to become a criminal at large, a dangerous and wanted man, he stooped down so that only the very top of his head could be seen through the windows of the car. The thought of what he was about to do made him laugh. He could already see their sergeant or captain, or whoever was over them, pacing back and forth in front of the four policemen (standing at attention, of course), telling them that they were being relieved of their bikes because of the seriousness of their offense. After all, having a set of keys stolen right out from under their noses was every bit as important as having one's service revolver taken away. He reached out for the first key. And if they knew it was me, he thought, and began snickering so hard he had to bring his hand back to cover his mouth and help collect himself. Finally he stopped laughing, but continued smiling at his really colossal joke, and eased his hand up to the nearest key chain. Oh boy, he thought, this is really gonna be somethin' great. This'll be the best thing that's ever happened before. I'm really gonna be somebody. And I'll keep the keys, too, so all the guys'll know that I done it.

He smiled to himself and felt a warm wave of satisfaction pass over him. The feeling made him whole, a really complete and fulfilled person. It had been a long time since he had felt so wonderful. Once before he had triumphed over the old, big people, but that time, as good as it was, hadn't given him anything like the flashing, glowing, inspiring feeling that now moved through his body. Maybe this was so much better because he had thought of it all by himself without Earl hanging around to correct his thinking and suggest better ways. This was entirely his show and he was determined to bring it off with all the finesse of an experienced pickpocket—and without Earl standing by and taking all the credit after it was finished and he stood on the school steps dangling four sets of keys for the older boys to see.

The other time, the time when he had felt almost as good, he and Earl had saved six firecrackers and gone to some length planning their big bang. The hardest part of the plan, of course, was saving them until the time was right. They had decided that their joke (actually three jokes with two firecrackers each —stems twisted together so they would go off at approximately the same time—for each of their three least favorite people on the block) would be most effective if they waited until the end of August so their unsuspecting victims would have forgotten about the tricks sometimes played on the Fourth of July. Seven weeks they saved them, and they were tempted to weaken, to light them and be done with it, at least fourteen times a week during that long frustrating period of time.

But the appointed time came and they set them all off that Saturday morning. First, Mrs. Hanson, the eighth-grade teacher who lived on the block and rode herd over them even when they were out of school. ("What are you boys doing with those cigarettes in your mouths?" "Wilford, I know your mother doesn't know you use language like that." "Earl, if I see you throw another rock at the school windows I'll see to it that you spend the rest of your life in your present grade.") She answered the door, heard the bang, and was so frightened she stepped on her glasses after they fell from the bridge of her long, sagging, curving nose.

Then Mr. Wallace, the old man who was retired and sat on his porch with a pan of hot water by his side and threw the water on them when they ran over his lawn following the path that had been there ever since they could remember. He was awakened from his afternoon nap by an explosion that startled him so he fell out of his chair. And when the ambulance came that night and took him to the hospital!—that was the funniest thing they had ever seen. They were relieved, however, when he came home the next day, still just as crabby and mean as ever.

And then Fred Jenkins, the machine, whom they knew they never would like because he didn't like little children, was so jarred by the double explosion—one a fraction after the first— that he even got up from his stool and looked out the door to see who had thrown the things into his store.

Yeah, Wilford said to himself, that was somethin' all right, but nothin' like this'll be. And I'm doin' it all by myself, too, without that runt Earl and without nobody. He snickered so hard that his whole body shook from excitement. He turned the ignition off and waited to see if anyone would notice the absence of one-twelfth of the noise. He peeked through the windows of the car. No, they hadn't noticed how quiet it had become where he stood. He began easing the key out of the lock, slowly, as if this sound, too, might be discerned.

"Wilford!"

He jumped up straight, letting go of the key, which slid from the lock and dropped to the street. He spun around on his heels, looking for the person who belonged to the young voice, terrified, his heart pounding now even louder than a moment ago, his head spinning, his vision blurred. He could see no one.

"Wilford! What's hapnin', man?" Earl said, stepping out from behind a parked car up the street.

Wilford sighed, relieved. Then he was flowing with anger again. But this time it was a boy's anger directed at a friend who had just rescued him from becoming a wanted man but had still managed to ruin the best plan he had ever had. Wilford had a right to be angry. "*Earl, you . . . you . . .*" He slapped his thigh in frustration, threw both hands in the air, and began hurrying across the street.

"Hey," Earl said.

Wilford was over the curb now. "What!"

"Where you goin'?"

Into the vacant lot. Oooo, that Earl, he thought. "For a walk," he said angrily.

"Where to, man?" Earl said, trotting to catch up.

At the rear of the lot, turning into the alley. Every time I do somethin', he thought, here comes Earl. Just one time—just one time I'd like to do somethin' without him poppin' up and messin' it all up. Ooooo, would I like to let him have it, pow! He looked back at Earl, without breaking his stride and shouted, "Nowhere!"

"Well, wait up. I'll go with you."

Earl caught up with him in the alley. "Whatja so mad about?" he asked.

Wilford stepped up his pace and refused to answer.

"Well?" Earl insisted.

Wilford kicked a tin can and when it stopped bouncing he ran up and kicked it again.

"Boy, are you mad. I ain't seen you that mad since that time your ole girl friend Joyce slapped your face. You was steamin' that time, too. Man, were you steamin'."

"She ain't my girl friend."

"Oh yes she is. I saw that note you wrote her. She showed it to the whole room. Icchh, what a mushy note."

"I didn't write no letter to Joyce and not to nobody else, either."

"Yes, sir. Yes you did, 'cause you didn't spell 'dearest' right. And I bet you can't spell it now, either."

"I sure too can spell it, and I didn't write her and she ain't my girl friend." He picked up a rock and threw it at a bottle, missing by six feet.

Earl threw with more precision, bouncing the rock off the thick sides of the bottle.

They stopped walking.

"Bet you can't kick this can as far as I can," Wilford said.

"That's a bet."

"Okay. You go first."

Earl set the can on its end, backed up a few steps, ran toward it, and sent it bouncing down the alley a distance of about thirty feet.

Wilford took another can from a pile of garbage. Next he found a rock and leaned the can back against the rock like a football. Then he backed up five paces, jumped up, and began advancing on the can. His foot connected and sent rock and can into the air. The can soared in a perfect spiral at least fifteen feet beyond Earl's can. Then it landed and bounced and rolled another ten feet. Wilford smiled and began walking again.

Earl looked up at him, smiled, shook his head in satisfaction, and walked along with him. Then he picked up a rock and threw it up the alley at a rat that was roaming over a mound of garbage. The rock missed the rat by inches but stirred up enough garbage to cause it to squeak in terror and burrow deep into the mound and out of sight before they had reached it.

"Hey, man," Earl said. "Why didn't you come by this mornin'?"

"I don't know. Guess I just wanted to be by myself. I looked over at your window. Shades was down. Figured you was sleepin', I guess. I don't know."

"*Man*, it sure rained last night."

"Yeah," Wilford said. "Ain't seen it rain like that in a long time." And then he could avoid it no longer. "Did you see the way they shot him?" he said looking straight ahead up the alley.

Earl cleared his throat nervously. "No, no. I didn't see it. Ah, the lightnin'. Remember the lightnin'?"

"Yeah."

"Well . . ." He paused, ashamed to admit to a weakness. "When that streak of lightnin' hit, I closed my eyes as tight as I could. Next thing I knew the door flew open and knocked me down. I thought sure lightnin' had hit the door. I crawled under the stool. When I looked out the door, man, people was goin' at it and fightin' all over the place and then the cops was everywhere and people was hollerin' and I cut out the back door of Mr. Frank's store and *flew* home, man. I ain't never seen nothin' like what folks was doin'. You ever see that many folks fightin' before?"

Wilford shook his head. "'cept in the movies and on television. That's the only time, I guess."

"You saw 'em shoot him, huh?"

"Yeah," Wilford said, nodding his head slowly.

They reached the end of the block, came out of the alley, stopped at the street waiting for traffic to clear, and then went on into the next block, another alley with more cans and bottles and rocks and garbage and rats.

"Whatja gonna do?" Earl asked.

"The older guys told me not to tell nobody nothin'.'"

"What if the cops come by and ask you?"

"What for?"

"You know—to be a witness."

"Oh. I don't know. Guess I won't tell 'em."

Earl smiled. "That's smart. My old man said not to even tell 'em I was in the store if they ask. He said just say, 'I don't know nothin', Mister,' and that's all. He said the best thing to do—in somethin' like this—is to just keep outta it. He says it ain't none of my business and don't say nothin' to nobody—not even you."

"Yeah, I guess that's right."

They began kicking cans again, selecting new ones when the ones they were kicking went out of bounds into someone's yard or on the roof of a garage. When they reached the end of the block they turned out of the alley and walked along the sidewalk under the shade of the elevated tracks overhead, looking into windows of the businesses on this their most successful business street in the neighborhood.

They stopped to listen to the music coming from a juke box in a tavern that had just opened. Wilford leaned against the plate-glass window of the tavern the way he had seen drunks do so often (and they never fell through, either). "You know, Earl, it's a good thing you didn't see it because it was bad. I don't think you could take it, Earl. I mean, you see, it was *real* bad. You little guys are tough, all right, but that was *real* bad. Man, that was *real* bad." He shook his head from side to side and sighed. "Oh, man, it was real, *real* bad."

"I know," Earl said sadly.

Wilford had expected an argument. He was looking forward to it. When it didn't come, he shrugged his shoulders and continued walking; heading past the many taverns and chicken shacks, past the barbecue houses, the store-front churches, the record shops, the second-hand furniture stores, the one pawnshop, the two hamburger stands, the funeral parlor, the hardware store, the beauty parlors and barbershops, the gas station, the radio and T.V. repair shop, the shoe shop, the ladies' hat shop, the drugstore, the poolroom, the grocery store, the laundromats, the cleaning shops, the jewelry stores, the jewelry stores that were also pawnshops and buyers of stolen jewelry, and more and still more taverns, until they finally arrived at the Pepsi-Cola plant, where they stood looking through the open window; watching the machines preparing the soft drinks for market, and drooling and wanting a drink and daydreaming that someone would come out and give them one.

"The inquest will please come to order," the Deputy Coroner said dryly. He was a heavy man, overweight, with gray hair, and glasses that rode back down his nose as soon as he had taken his hand off them. He was a part-time doorbell pusher, a full-time hand-shaking precinct captain, a day-and-night card-carrying party member, a monthly dues payer, an annual eater of unsold tickets to the political fund-raising event. He was old, wrinkled, weary from thousands of favors done to and for and by the system. He was a great manipulator of decisions, an organizer of classic cover-ups that the whole city could see but chose to overlook for fear that when their time came for a favor the do-gooders would close the doors on them. He was one of the guardians of this happy stage of political evolution and he was bored because he had already heard two cases and he wanted to get out and join a political foursome on the golf course.

He hadn't broken one hundred all year, but he had made many contacts and renewed a few old friendships that could prove to be important to him in years to come. Once or twice this summer he had been briefed by a lawyer about an upcoming inquest in which the lawyer's client was being held for murder and, like some really efficient lawyers, he felt it was better to win the case before the hearing, or at least have what appeared to be an inevitable murder verdict reduced to manslaughter.

One of these briefings had concerned a very difficult case

indeed, and even though the Deputy had already been paid two hundred dollars to deliver a verdict of justifiable homicide, it was necessary after the first hearing to meet with the lawyer and impress upon him the importance of lining up three persons who would swear they were present and were witnesses and saw the victim attack the defendant first, with a knife in his hand.

The case had started out fairly simply, but took a turn for the worse when two witnesses testified that the defendant beat the victim with a pistol and then shot him. They also testified that they did not see a weapon in the victim's hand. The Deputy didn't want to return the money, and he wouldn't have, even if the lawyer had not produced three manufactured witnesses. The verdict of the coroner's jury, of course, after three such distinguished witnesses (one of them well on his way to being drunk two hours before noon), was justifiable homicide, but it might not have come off if he had not had that eighteen-hole meeting out in the good clean fresh air of the suburbs away from the perpetual grit-cloud of Chicago.

He didn't have such a meeting this day, but he could never tell when he might meet someone of importance: a clerk in an office who might be of some use to him, or a ward committeeman or an alderman or a judge's bailiff, or maybe, if he was lucky, a state senator who was on his way up in the organization.

He was bored with inquests and wanted to change jobs, so he needed all the contacts he could get. It seemed to him that he had been hearing inquests half of his life. They were so routine now.

"This is the first hearing of an inquest into the death of one Nathaniel Hamilton. It's case number seventy-five of August of this year," he said, with such complete indifference that his boredom was obvious to everyone present. The whole business of conducting inquests was a waste of time to him, and

Cornbread was just another lifeless thing that stood in the way of his going to the golf course in time to meet some really important people. Cornbread was another meaningless cadaver to be ripped open by one of the coroner's physicians, exposing insides that looked routinely like the insides of every other unfortunate, cold, lifeless body in the basement.

With him, every case was routine, unless a witness or a fellow party member or a lawyer for one of the participants, before or even during the hearing, leaned closer to the Deputy and confided thus:

THE PERSON: Timothy Brady sends his regards to you.

THE DEPUTY: Timothy Brady *himself?* The *congressman?*

THE PERSON: The very same Timothy Francis Brady.

THE DEPUTY: And you know him well, do you?

THE PERSON: As well as I know my very own hand, I know him.

THE DEPUTY: No. You don't say!

THE PERSON: All his married life, and even before that I know him. It's my third cousin's sister-in-law he's married to.

THE DEPUTY: God, man. Why didn't you tell me he was your kin?

The room was twenty-five by fifty. The Deputy Coroner sat on a raised platform (how mighty justice appears when it can look down—God!) behind a steel-and-formica desk that formed the top of a T with another metal-and-formica table filling in the long shaft. To the left and right of him were chairs; on the left, beneath his mighty platform, were ten chairs, side by side, stopping at the double doors (one of which was always locked for no reason at all); on the right, two rows of three chairs each (two raised platforms, one even higher than the Deputy's!) wherein the jurors (six of them, all past retirement age, working to aid the cause of justice because it gets them out of the house and pays two dollars and sixty cents a case) sit fidgeting, occasionally napping, eating hard candy and sometimes, when the witnesses speak exceptionally loud, listening to the testimony.

The Deputy yawned. "The decedent came to his death as a result of a supposed attempted robbery and resisting arrest and was shot during the pursuit. The investigating officers are present?"

A police officer seated along the wall holding a folder stuffed with many typewritten papers on his lap answered: "Yes, sir."

The Deputy now raised his eyes and looked at the officer for the first time. "Is there a member of the family present?"

"Yes, sir. They are present. The mother and father are both here."

"All right. And are all of your witnesses here and are we ready to go ahead with this case today?"

"Well, Mr. Coroner, there ain't no witnesses except the two policemen and they're both still in the hospital because of what happened after the shooting."

"You better explain for the record what you mean by that, Officer."

"Yes, sir. After the suspect was shot by Officers Golich and Atkins, for resisting arrest, the people out in that neighborhood jumped them and beat up on them. The officers sustained injuries that required that they be hospitalized—serious injuries."

"You say serious. I assume they're not critical?"

"Well, they're critical enough, Mr. Coroner."

"I don't mean that way," he said roughly. "Are they on the critical list? Is there any chance that they might die as a result of the beating they received?"

"Oh, no. They were serious, but they weren't critical. I didn't know what you meant, sir." He smiled to hide his embarrassment. "I'm sorry. I didn't understand you."

The Deputy softened slightly. "That's all right, Officer. And they were the only witnesses, did you say?"

"Yes, sir."

"Well, we'll go as far as we can. If we can close it out without them being here, we will. If not—and I don't see how we can close it out today—we'll just have to continue it until they get out of the hospital and we can have them here to tell us what happened." He shuffled through his papers and found the sheet that contained the names of the jurors; the all-important pay sheet, it was called by the jurors. "I'll have a roll call of the jury," he said. Then he read the first name, making a check mark by it and moving onto the next name without waiting for the automatic "here," from the responding juror, so that one juror was answering as he was calling the name of the next. When he had finished the roll call he began signing the many sheets for the coroner's statistical files, all of which required his signature in the lower right-hand corner. As he signed the sheets he went through another formality.

"Are you gentlemen acquainted with the deceased or any member of the family of the deceased?"

Two of the jurors answered. One remained silent because he had not heard the question. He would hear very little of the unfolding testimony because his hearing had begun to slip earlier that year and the lack of money and the excess of male ego worked against his ever buying a hearing aid. And when the inquest was closed and the jurors retired to their private room to deliberate (joined within seconds by the Deputy, who would suggest the verdict before any of those who listened had a chance to present their opinion of the case), he would agree with whatever the Deputy said. If one of the new men had ideas about the case that conflicted with that of the Deputy, the sleeper would put him in his place by saying: "The Deputy's been hearing these cases for years. He knows what the verdict should be."

The other three jurors didn't answer because they were the most experienced and knew no one was interested in their an-

53

swers and it was always assumed that their answers, if they had troubled themselves to speak out, would, of course, be the right ones.

"Is there any reason why, after you've heard the testimony presented here, is there any reason why you cannot deliver to me, the Deputy Coroner of this county, a fair and just verdict?"

"No, sir," the two men answered.

"Are there any objections to these men serving as jurors?"

There was no reply from the lawyer who sat at the end of the long table facing the Deputy. He knew it was useless to object. He would have to contain himself. An objection at this time would have no meaning.

"All right," the Deputy said, now rearranging his papers so that he could move into the next phase of the inquest. "Hearing no objections, let the record indicate that the jurors were sworn in over the body of the deceased here at the Cook County Morgue." He moved his pen up to the line that was reserved for the names of lawyers who were present at the hearing. "Are there any legal representatives present today?" he asked.

"Yes, sir," the dapper young lawyer answered, with a warm smile and a slight nod of his head that he used when his instant charm was needed. He knew it would be a difficult case for him and that he could get nowhere if he antagonized the Deputy, so he was prepared to charm him and hope that that way he might be allowed to go into some detail and, with a little luck, provoke a few admissions from the police that would aid him later on in the civil case the family of the deceased was going to bring against the City of Chicago and the two police officers. He was dressed in a dark-brown suit with subdued chalk stripes and a vest. The brown of the suit matched his skin perfectly. He wore a black tie and a brown pastel button-down shirt. His wing-tip shoes were shined and there was a smudge on his left toe where someone had backed into him on the elevator riding up to the twenty-first floor to his office earlier that morning. He had meant to wipe off the shoe before he left the office, but he became involved with another of the young lawyers in his office, overjoyed at hearing that there were witnesses, and had forgotten this slight imperfection in his dress. His woolly hair was scented with an expensive oil and well brushed, and gave the appearance of always being freshly cut. He was close-shaven. His eyes were brown and squinted slightly when he smiled. He wore thick-rimmed glasses. His nose was broad, his lips were full. He had an oval face that was neither handsome nor ugly, and he beamed with personality and the kind of professionalism the Deputy had not seen for a long time.

"My name, Mr. Coroner, is Benjamin Blackwell," he said with an Oxford accent that startled and temporarily paralyzed the Deputy.

Oh Jesus, the Deputy said to himself. It's not bad enough that I got to have a lawyer on this damn case. Oh, shit, it's gonna be a rotten day. I get one of these smart ones—one of these smart nigger lawyers. Got a funny feeling about this damn case, dammit. Better play it close.

"I'm here in behalf of the family of the deceased, Mr. Coroner. I'm here in behalf of Mr."—he paused, nodding slightly —"and Mrs. Jefferson Hamilton. And if I may, Mr. Coroner, I'd like to set the record straight by advising the coroner—"

"What's your address, Counsel?"

"My address, sir, is 111 West Washington Street, Suite 2100."

"What's your telephone number there?"

"Franklin 2-1106."

The Deputy scribbled the last four digits and looked up into the smiling face of Mr. Blackwell.

"May I continue with my statement now, Mr. Coroner?"

"Yes. Yes. What did you want to say?"

"Thank you, sir. I was about to say that I'd like to set the record straight and inform the Coroner and the distinguished jurors that I have come into certain information today, through a telephone conversation with an associate of mine, that indicates there were, in fact, several witnesses to this foul act— this most foul act."

"What?" the Deputy said angrily.

"That is correct. To be exact, there were at least three persons who had been in the company of the young man only seconds before he was murdered and have personal knowledge of this incident."

The police officer jumped to his feet. "Mr. Coroner, is he calling me a liar?"

"Just a minute," the Deputy said.

"I am not at this time calling you a liar, Officer; however, if you do not investigate this case thoroughly, I may well yet be forced to call you that, yes. It wouldn't be the first time I've called someone a liar. And it surely wouldn't be the first time I've called a policeman a liar."

The court reporter sat behind his stenotype machine jerking his head from speaker to speaker as if it were necessary for him to see them to read their lips. He wrote furiously on his machine, angered that they were now all talking at the same time.

"Now just a minute," the Deputy said, throwing his ballpoint pen down on the desk. "Now listen to me, both of you. I want to get this straight right now so we'll have an understanding. I don't want any arguing between you. I'm running this inquest and I'll run it as I see fit."

Mr. Blackwell stood and bowed slightly. "Please accept my apologies, Mr. Coroner," he said, and then sat down again.

The Deputy smiled, picked up his pen, and nodded to Mr. Blackwell. "All right. But I want you to remember, Counsel, that you are here as a guest of the coroner."

"I understand that, sir, and I appreciate it."

"This is not a civil case and I don't want you to try to prove up your case here."

"I shall abide by your request, sir."

"All right. All right. That's enough of that, too."

Mr. Blackwell nodded.

"Now, Officer, you say there's no witnesses and he says there are. Do you know the people Counsel's talking about? Did you try to get witnesses?"

"Mr. Coroner, we've tried for days, but there aren't any witnesses out there. At least nobody wants to talk to us about it, anyways. We've been out there all over the neighborhood and nobody—not one single person came forth and said they were a witness. You know how it is out there, Mr. Coroner. We get no co-operation whatsoever. We *never* get any co-operation. So if he's got any witnesses, I don't know where he got 'em from."

"Counsel, did you give the names of your witnesses to the police department?"

"No, sir. I did not, Mr. Coroner. This is the first opportunity I've had to see the policeman. I assumed, Mr. Coroner, that as part of their investigation, they would make every effort to contact witnesses and would be aware of them."

The investigating officer, Patrick O'Kelly, six feet three inches tall, two hundred and sixty pounds of round-headed, freckled, slightly tanned, blue-eyed, beer-bellied, explosive, flush-faced anger, shuffled the papers on his lap nervously. The bottom of the folder opened and several sheets fell out, scattering as they struck the floor. He leaned forward to scoop up the papers and the blood rushing to his head turned an already bright face cherry red.

Mr. Blackwell thought: You poor dumb slob. I'll cut your lying heart to ribbons when I get you in court. If they don't put anybody any smarter than you on this case . . . He watched the awkward man trying with massive hands to raise one last piece of onionskin paper from the floor without benefit of fingernails. He tried not to wrinkle the paper, and as he slid his thumb against the edge, the paper almost defensively pressed tighter to the floor and his claw of a thumb slid over it repeatedly.

The Deputy was hypnotized by the combat between paper and man, and he watched with his glasses dropped, his mouth open, and his right hand exposing and retracting the point of the pen with an even, rhythmic click-click, click-click, click-click, click-click.

The jurors leaned forward in their seats to see what the officer was doing.

Mr. and Mrs. Hamilton sat on the first bench immediately behind their attorney and stared at the floor directly in front of them. They were not moved by the officer, or by the Coroner, or by anything that was happening here today. They sat in their seats, still numbed by their experience, and silently mourned their loss, unable to adjust to the finality of death.

O'Kelly, frustrated, embarrassed, and snorting like a bull about to charge, wrinkled the paper into his clenched fist, leaned on his other hand to slide back into the chair, got a cramp in his left forearm, let out just the slightest yell, and slid out of the seat onto his hands and knees.

The court reporter laughed out loud. The jurors snickered among themselves and the Deputy smiled. Mr. Blackwell shook his head. You poor dumb slob, he thought. I almost feel sorry for you. Look at him, the big dumb ass. He wouldn't know how to testify honestly if his life depended on it.

O'Kelly got to his feet, leaned over, felt behind him for the chair, found it, and sat down, brushing the knees of his pants off after he had organized the papers again, straightening out the wrinkled sheet.

"Are you settled now, Officer?" the Deputy asked.

"Yes, sir," answered Officer O'Kelly, wishing he could make himself smaller, so small that he would not be noticed by the littler people who always seemed to be making fun of him because of his clumsiness.

"Counsel is going to give you the names of the witnesses—you will give him the names, won't you, Counsel?" Mr. Blackwell nodded. "Fine. I thought you would. And you'll continue your investigation as you normally would; however, now you have these persons and you'll determine, after you investigate, I'm sure, whether or not these people were, in fact, witnesses to this occurrence. Is that understood?"

"Yes, sir."

Mr. Blackwell cleared his throat. "Just a minute, Mr. Coroner."

"What now?" the Deputy said disgustedly.

"Well, Mr. Coroner, I think it's really up to you and this jury to determine if these persons are, in fact, witnesses to this matter. This is not part of the investigative operation of the police department. This is not at all within their purview. It is entirely within the province of the coroner's office to call witnesses and, upon hearing said witnesses, to determine the validity of their testimony. And I would strongly object to giving the names of these persons to the police department unless they are to be brought here to testify before—"

"They're going to be brought in at the next hearing. That's what I just told him!"

The hell you did, Blackwell thought. I know what you told him. And he said, "Oh, I beg your pardon, Mr. Coroner. I didn't understand you. Then am I to understand that the police department, particularly Officer—what's your name, Officer?"

"O'Kelly."

"Officer O'Kelly here, is being charged with the responsibility

5 9

of apprising these witnesses of the next hearing date and seeing to it that they are present here at that time?"

"Yes! That's what I just told him," the Deputy said angrily. "Why don't you listen to what I say, Counsel."

"Please accept my apologies, Mr. Coroner."

"I just started to say that when you interrupted me. I want those witnesses in here. Now you go ahead with your investigation and find out what they know, of course, and take statements from them and whatever you have to do. And if you come upon any other witnesses, why, bring those in, too." He pushed his glasses back up his nose with his right hand and as he did it, the point of the pen just barely touched his skin leaving a blue line in the center of his forehead. "If I remember correctly—well, is this the case I read about in the paper the other day?"

"Yes, sir," Officer O'Kelly boomed out. "It's the one where they—"

"I know what they did," he growled. "I read it in the paper, I told you." He began working the mechanism of the pen again, his thumb moving faster this time. "This is the one where they ganged up on the policemen out there in that colored neighborhood . . ." (Blackwell thought: In court I'd object to all this as prejudicial to my client, but this isn't court. Good God! Any more institutions like this and we can forget the legal system.) ". . . where they have—where we get so many cases from." He searched his mind for the next sentence. The pen clicked on, aiding his thought process. "I just had a case from out there the other day—what was it?—we held four or five colored boys for murder—from that very same area out there. They beat the man to death. We have a lot of trouble out that way."

Mr. Blackwell leaned forward, resting his forehead in his open palms. Well, Blackwell, he thought, I guess that tells you where you stand in this case. Before they're through they'll have your client pointing the gun first at the policemen and then turning it on himself and committing suicide. Finally he spoke. "Mr. Coroner, I don't see what bearing that has on this case."

"What?" the Deputy said, looking at him as if he hadn't understood a word he said.

"Well, sir, to begin with, the beating was after the fact. In short, Mr. Coroner, my client—or the son of my client—was shot first by these two policemen. After this shooting, certain events led to the beating sustained by them. Now what happened after the decedent was shot has nothing to do with the actual occurrence about which we are concerned here today."

"I know that, Counsel! I'm just trying—I'm sitting here and I'm telling the officer something that I read in the newspapers. And if we could believe the newspapers, though I know this is not at all a good reference, I believe the *Trib* said this deceased boy was one of a gang and that the gang turned on the policemen after they had shot him. But that's not important here today. We'll find out what happened when we get the policemen here and put them on the witness stand and they tell their stories to this jury."

"And the witnesses," Mr. Blackwell said light-heartedly.

"Yes, of course."

"Yes, sir."

He shuffled through his papers, not looking for anything, just trying to buy some time as he thought about what to say next. He had to be cautious around lawyers. "Just thought I'd let you know that I'm prepared to go ahead if we have to because I do know something about the case."

Blackwell thought: I know *exactly* what you know. Whatever the police say is right. Rubber-stamp it and get it over with. I don't know why I'm wasting my time here. But I keep hoping. Yeah, I keep hoping that one of these days . . . And he said, nodding his head twice and smiling, "Yes, sir."

"But," the Deputy said (click-click, click-click, click-click), "there's no need to go into that today, is there? Because we won't be able to close the case out and I don't see any reason for taking any testimony today. I won't even put you on the stand, Officer. And I won't take the family history, either, Counsel, so your clients won't have to come up here yet. I'll do all that at the next hearing. I'll get the family history from them . . ." click-click, click-click, click-click ". . . at the next hearing when we have everybody here and can proceed from the beginning to the end without any interruption."

Goddamn, the court reporter thought, I wish he'd stop playing with that stupid pen. It was one of the many distractions he had had to condition himself to ignore, but at times even the most insignificant noises were colossal distractions when one was listening for every word that was spoken; and he knew that his dexterity or lack of it—after the case was several years old and forgotten and going to trial and the transcript was pulled out and scrutinized—would be the only thing of real importance because the record would be what everyone was depending on. Both sides would attempt to use it. Both sides knew the reporter was impartial, even though he was paid by the coroner's office. And both sides would read the record carefully, searching for flaws in the case of their opponent, and if there was anything in the transcript that would brighten their hopes, if there was anything that was questionable, if they had any indication that the reporter might have erred, they would call him in to testify, too, and tear the record apart page by page, hoping to prove his incompetency.

But for someone so important, he was the most neglected man in the hearing. They talked at the same time. They interrupted each other. They went on as fast as they could, as if they didn't know he was there struggling with ten fingers and his little stenotype machine to record their sounds accurately and in their proper sequence. Indeed, they often forgot him.

Why shouldn't they? He was perfect. He never made mistakes. He was like the machine he used, they thought. But they didn't know that the machine was only as dependable as the man who used it. They didn't know that he was often at his breaking point. They didn't know that he had come to work this day with a pair of hands that refused to type with the dexterity required of them and had to be forced to move, had to be almost literally whipped all the way through the case. The court reporter sighed, relieved that the case was not going to proceed now and that his day of taking shorthand had ended. Perhaps his hands would work better at the typewriter when he got back to the office and transcribed some of the cases piled on his desk.

He dropped his hands from the machine and rested while one of the jurors went to the front desk to get the continuance book so the Deputy could pick a suitable date for all concerned. It was recess, even if the Deputy didn't so designate when he said to the juror, "Will you get the continuance book?" The reporter had not written that because it had no place in the transcript. It was one of the many things that would never have been said on the record in a courtroom. But these hearings were not conducted by trained personnel. They were conducted by precinct captains who had been told by other deputies in a half-dozen or so quick lessons what they should do and how to go about it; other precinct captains with no background in the law, other precinct captains who held these choice positions because they were required to work only half of the day and they could devote the rest of the day to another field of endeavor that earned them as much if not more money. And they had no concept of how one should handle oneself in the presence of a man trained to write instinctively, reacting catlike to the sound of words, gently but swiftly pouncing upon the keys and recording sounds that would, at a later date, be transformed into words on the printed page.

The reporter had written "Short recess," lowered his hands, and rested. He was happy that the day of taking testimony was almost over.

The juror returned with the appointment book.

"All right," the Deputy said. "Let's see now. What would be a good date? What do you think we ought to do, Officer? You think we should set a date, say, about three weeks from now?"

"I think that would be a good idea, Mr. Coroner, 'cause you can't—they ain't going to be out before then, I'm pretty sure."

"Well, now, are they that bad off?"

"Yes, sir." He nodded his crew-cut head. "They're both in pretty bad shape."

"Well . . ." He fumbled through pages of scribbling. ". . . maybe we ought to, say, give them enough time to get well." Click-click, click-click, click-click. "How about the end of September? How's that fit in with your schedule?"

"That's all right."

"Seems to me that ought to be long enough. Now if they get well a lot before that, why, you call me and I'll set it up to another date. No, on second thought, we better leave it set for that date in September at the end of the month, say, the twenty-fourth of September. How's that with you, Counsel?"

"That's fine with me, Mr. Coroner. Either the twenty-third of the month or the twenty-fourth would be all right with me."

"No. We'll leave it at the twenty-fourth of September at one o'clock, right back here in this room with me."

"That's fine, Mr. Coroner," the officer said. "And I'll see those witnesses and we'll have time to finish our investigation, too, now that you gave us that much more time."

Mr. Blackwell nodded.

"Now, Officer, if either one of those officers should, heaven forbid, die as a result of this occurrence, you let me know and we'll tie that death in with this one."

"Okay."

"And I hope—well, you say they're not on the critical list, don't you?"

"That's right, sir. They're both in good shape—well, they ain't in good shape, but they're out of danger and they're going to live."

"Yeah. Okay, then, this case is continued to September 24, 1965, at one o'clock, right back here at the Cook County Morgue. That's all for today."

The six jurors got up, almost as one unit, and began moving slowly toward the door behind the Deputy, discussing baseball and the marital habits, as presented to them through the newspapers, of certain movie stars. They went into the jury room, leaving the door open, and they could be heard arguing about batting averages and games won and lost.

"Just a minute," the Deputy said to the officer. "I want to talk to you before you leave."

Officer O'Kelly had stood and turned toward the other door and was about to take a step. Upon command, he turned and walked to the Deputy's desk and stopped in front of him with his mouth open, waiting for the Deputy to speak.

The Deputy looked agitatedly at Mr. Blackwell, who was still seated.

O'Kelly tried to be patient, but he was hungry and he quickly tired of waiting. "Yes, sir," he said, hoping to jar the Deputy back to him and force him to speak so he could get out and have his lunch and a tall glass of beer.

Blackwell busied himself with the papers in front of him. He knew they were going to discuss the case and he wanted to eavesdrop. It wasn't a gentlemanly thing to do, but he felt he wasn't fighting against gentlemen.

The Deputy shifted nervously in his seat. Click-click, click-click. "Counsel, the case is over."

"I know," said Mr. Blackwell. "I'm just checking my notes."

"Well, do you mind checking them outside. I have another case I want to discuss with the police officer."

"Oh . . . sure, Mr. Coroner. I'm sorry." And he thought: Well, that didn't work, but it doesn't matter. I know what they're going to talk about. He placed his papers in the brief-case and got to his feet. "Good-by, Mr. Coroner. See you on the twenty-fourth, unless I have another case out here before then."

God! I hope not, the Deputy thought. "Yes, yes. Good-by. Good-by, Counsel," he said, rushing him on. "Take your people with you, please."

"Yes. Of course." Mr. Blackwell made a sweeping motion with his left hand and bowed slightly and Mr. and Mrs. Hamilton followed the direction of his hand and preceded him through the door.

The Deputy waited until he was sure they were not going to return. Then he turned to face Officer O'Kelly, pointed the pen at him, and said, "What the hell you guys think you're doing bringing a case over here when there're witnesses and saying there ain't no witnesses? Huh?"

"Mr. Coroner, if I—"

"Now goddammit, I'm tired of this. You guys know damn well we'll cover for you if it's at all possible—we have to—we have to cover for each other—but if he comes in here with three witnesses who were with that kid and they say anything other than what I read in the papers—you're dead. Now what's he talking about? Was this thing like the papers said? How can there be witnesses that you don't know anything about? I don't like the looks of this case. Is there something about it that I should know?"

"Mr. Coroner, I don't know anything about witnesses. If I had any I would 'f brought 'em in. I told you exactly what the situation is out there. You can't get them damn niggers to cooperate. You know that. We can't get 'em to even talk to us. Even the informants won't talk since we had that riot out there."

"Riot? What riot?"

"It was a riot all right. The papers didn't know about it because we clamped down on it before it could spread."

"You mean the *papers* didn't know about it?"

"Well, they knew, but when they called the station the captain told 'em it was a gang."

"And they bought *that?*"

"Sure. Well, you know where it is: you know the neighborhood, don't you?" Then without waiting for a reply, "That's our sin corner out there," he said, confident that he had moved into a position of some eminence and could now sit back in comfort and tell the Deputy a thing or two. "Once the old man told 'em there were two policemen injured and that we were flooding the area to try to apprehend the offenders, the rest of this Nathaniel Hamilton's gang, they dropped it. They wrote their stories around that."

"But it wasn't a gang, or was it? You say it was a riot?"

"That's right, it was a *riot*. It might have been a gang, too, but it was really just spon—spon—spontaneous. Them niggers are really getting out of hand out there. We've got the whole area under real tight coverage. I'll be glad when they tear all them damn buildings down so we can get some peace out there."

"Well," click-click, "I'll be damned. Well, at any rate, you better find out about those witnesses. There's no chance that these were a couple of trigger-happy cops, is there?"

"Oh, no, sir. They're both good men."

"Are they white? Are they colored?"

"Well, one's white and one's colored. The colored boy's been on the force eight years and the white guy's been on about four. They've been partners for quite a while. I think the old man said they were the fifth team of colored and white in the district—or was it in the city? Well, they're the fifth team somewheres and they've been having some pretty good results. They're well known out there. But they're not a couple of rookies."

"Okay. It's good that they're not both white. At least we don't have that goddamn racial angle. I guess that's why we didn't have any of those civil rights people here. God! That's all I'd need is to have a few of them in here tearing the place up and shouting and falling out all over the place. A bunch of 'em were out here last year on a case of mine and I don't want to see the likes of them again for a long time. But at least we don't have that to worry about on this case. I'm tired of sticking my neck out when it's not worth it. If there's anything wrong about this case and you haven't told me about it, so help me—"

"No, no, Mr. Coroner. I told you everything. Everything we know about it, anyway. They're just upset because nobody wants to believe that this kid, this boy Cornbread or Nathaniel, was in with the bad element out there. See, he was some kind of star athlete in school and he was supposed to have a lot of scholarships and he was due to leave next month for school and nobody knew about this side of his life. We questioned all of our informants and they didn't even know. But there's nothing wrong. It's just that they can't take it. You know how those people are. They can't take it when things go against them."

"Okay, but you better be right, or so help me I'll let it go and let the feathers fly. But you see that you get to those witnesses and find out what they know and if they say something that's going to change things—well, you just get to those witnesses and see what they have to say. I'll see you next month."

"Okay, Mr. Coroner. But I'll probably be back a helluva lot more before then—the way they kill each other out there."

"Okay. But just you make sure you don't leave me holding it, because—like I said—I'm tired of sticking my neck out for nothing. You guys know we'll cover for you any time we can, but if this thing gets too hot—well, there's nothing I can do."

"Yes, sir."

Part Two

■

They came to Chicago forty, fifty years ago like a school of black minnows frantically dashing away from danger; running to the great symbol of freedom up North, where they could be treated almost like human beings. Any improvement would be better than the state of enslavement they had left in the forgotten, vicious parts of Mississippi, Georgia, Alabama, Tennessee, and Louisiana. They came almost straight up to the center of the country, bursting with industry, screaming to the world that it needed hands and minds and souls to help it grow; singing to the world about equality and freedom and employment and housing and hospitals and churches and women and booze and food! They came up from the deep, deep, dead, hidden valleys of the South and they shouldered their way in and mingled with the foreigners and fought the aliens for jobs, and won the jobs as they won the negative respect of the established citizens. They squeezed their way as close to the existing social structure as they were allowed to go, and then they settled back and prospered and raised children and taught their children not to fight, not to resist, but to accept their limited progress as the end of the evolutionary pattern. They grew weak and mellowed from their success, and their children never developed hearts or shoulders or minds, and were gutless.

Their children refused to involve themselves with trivial things like politics or social improvements and pulled in the fences that surrounded their tiny ranch houses. Their children tightened the requirements for entrance into their sick social clubs. At first they only wanted light skin and straight hair. Then they added a college degree to the light skin and straight hair. Then they added a minimum salary. Then they added the possession of a Buick. Then they added the Cadillac. They had arrived; they had reached the top of their limited world and they were scared shitless.

And when they lost their will to fight, they lost their progress, and sank beneath the high levels their parents had attained. And since they were incapable of fighting, incapable of resisting oppression, totally defenseless in the face of opposition, they just sat there and waited for someone to pull them back up.

And then in the 'forties and 'fifties a new wave of proud black men invaded Chicago. They came over the same sets of tracks as their forerunners, and they came just as penniless. They came with one suit of clothes and a shopping bag dangling from each hand. They came to the Polk Street station and they were dirty and poor and black. They were not light-skinned and they didn't have straight hair and they spoke like Southerners in their slow, sometimes loud, imperfect way, and their black brothers with seniority and the desire to be white were ashamed of them and ignored them and ran, ran, ran away from them and hid behind their cyclone and redwood fences, behind the security of their Martinis and social clubs. So the new immigrants first clustered in old areas that were being vacated by their brothers who had established themselves and were moving, now, into their own homes farther out south that white people were vacating in their flight to the suburbs. And once they had filled up these small areas on the south side, they began to assault the massive rambling west side of Chicago, as one hundred black people a day fled the inhuman South and journeyed to the Chicago of their dreams, to the Chicago that no longer had jobs for blacks, but would now rather substitute public aid than fair employment.

They came by the thousands and quadrupled the black population within less than twenty years. They came and pried their way into the city of no shoulders, into the vicious, lying, deceiving, corrupt Chicago that tried to deny their existence. But these people were not like the children of the giants. These people were hungry and they were alive. They wanted to see the Chicago of their dreams and they were willing to fight for it. They were ill informed and they were loud and they were sometimes vulgar, and sometimes they didn't have much respect for the law because the law had no respect at all for them, but they were vibrant with a will to belong and they were not afraid to fight for what they knew to be their right to remake Chicago.

But their opposition was even greater than that of the founders of the city, and their ultimate mastery of it will be longer in coming. When it does come the city will be a richer place; it will be the place poets dreamed of, it will be a place with free people, and it will breathe again, it will be alive.

■

It was four days before Larry Atkins opened his eyes and the doctor sighed and drew three lines through the word "critical" on his chart. During those four days he had many visitors; people he had not heard from in years. They came out of friendship for him. They came out of respect for his wife. And they came because of a genuine desire to give something of themselves. People read about his condition in the paper and many of them sent get-well cards and still more called the hospital to check on the progress of his recovery. Strangers, all strangers to him, who had been moved by his misfortune; fellow citizens who could never really be counted on, but who also could not be discounted because when they were touched, when they could be truly moved to the point of imagining themselves in similar circumstances, they would respond.

But those who knew him best came to offer their condolences for the death of his spirit; to mourn the loss of a man who had once been an idealist, but who had mellowed, as a man often does because of the security that money and position bring, or because he weakens and allows the system to overcome him and consume and destroy the dreams that are rebellious in nature and have no place in a patent, sterile society. Hidden beneath a firm crust—layers upon protective layers of bitterness and self-hate—brought about by his acceptance of the way of life he had chosen, of the middle-class standards, there still remained a slight flicker of the flame of rebellion. But so well hidden was his idealism, his constructive anger, his belief in his fellow man, that even he was not aware of it. They had come, these select few, who knew how devoted he had been to the old neighborhood, and wept inwardly for the death of his dream.

The dream was that when he finished school next year he would return to the old neighborhood and teach in the very same school where he had received his basic education and be the kind of teacher he knew the children needed. He had been on the police force eight years. He had attended night school the last six of those eight years. So many times he had been tempted to quit, but always he and his wife would find a way to get the tuition together, and she would urge him on and he would battle his way through another quarter.

She was a clever woman, his Beatrice. Often, when he was really down, she would trick him into believing that his mere presence had so stimulated her that she couldn't resist him and would all but plead with him to take her, to make wild, painful love to her although she seldom derived any pleasure from it, and with her body and her soft words and gentle sounds she would bring him out of his depression and transform him into a sedated but determined man of purpose. But sometimes loving and being loved was not enough for someone as sensitive as Larry, and she would have to resort to other means. Occasionally she would pick a fight, deliberately, to get his mind off what was bothering him. Sometimes it worked; sometimes it only made life more unbearable for both of them. But she was always trying, always truly concerned, always pushing, ready to aid their future in any way she could. Sometimes she played what she knew to be a game, the "professional game," she called it. And although Larry never knew he was the object of his wife's game, he was moved by it and profited and was pulled back in a safe direction. "When you become a teacher," she'd say, "I'll be so proud of you I'll come by the school every day and look up at your classroom and stop people on the street and say: 'That's my husband's room up there.' And they'll look at me and think I'm crazy, but I won't care because you'll be up there and we'll have made it." He'd grumble something about the price of textbooks and she'd touch his arm, or the slight bald spot at the back of his head, sigh, and say, "Larry Atkins, a teacher? This I can't believe. I'll have to see it first."

Larry Atkins—a teacher? he would say to himself in disbelief. It never sounded right, but that was the idea the children of his old neighborhood had planted after he had been on the force only two years. He had never thought of himself as being smart enough to get through college, but once he started he found he could pass, although it took a great deal of extra work and concentration on his part. He could pass, and on rare occasions when everything broke right he could even make the Dean's list.

When he came home from the Navy at the end of the Korean War his only plans for the future were to marry Beatrice and get a job and buy a home out on the far south side of Chicago where the people weren't forced to live so close together. They would have children and their children would play in their own yard. Larry would build a barbecue pit in that yard. They would have friends over and drink Martinis and eat barbecue and laugh as loud as they wanted to and play the record player as loud as it would go and no one could say anything to him about it. And most important: it would be his. He would personally own a piece of the city; some of the country he called home would indeed be home because it would be his.

When he got home he found that strange things had happened in Chicago. He found that many jobs were open to him that had been restricted to whites before he left for the service three years earlier. Of the jobs he considered, the police force seemed to offer two things the others lacked: a suitable pension plan that could be put into effect long before he reached the old age of sixty-five, and a position of respect in the community that meant he would be able to get credit and arrange for a loan with little difficulty. So he became a policeman and was stationed in the district where he had grown up and at that time still lived.

Within eighteen months he and Beatrice had saved enough money for a down payment (so modest that they still required a second mortgage) on a six-room house in a neighborhood that was in transition. They were lucky to get the house at such a low price. The owner was anxious to sell, because, as he told Larry: "I got three girls, and all of their little girl friends have moved, and you know how girls are. You're getting a good buy. I just paneled the back of the basement and the carpet stays and the storm windows. But I've got to sell quick because the place I want in the suburbs—the guy says he'll only hold it off the market a little longer. So I don't want to rush you, but if you can arrange it with the bank, we'll deal direct and cut out the real estate man and you can have it for fifteen even."

Beatrice was seven months pregnant at the time and it was so much pleasure to think that she would be able to have her baby and take it home to her own house and not the tiny two-room apartment full of cockroaches and bedbugs and memories of apartments she had lived in all her life, that she left the men, returned to the car, and cried warm tears of a kind of ecstasy she had never known before this minute.

Larry had driven halfway down the block, rushing to get to the bank before it closed, talking rapidly about the infinite advantages of this house and how lucky they were to be one of the first Negro families on that particular block, before he noticed that she was crying.

He stopped the car quickly. "Are you all right?" he asked anxiously.

"Oh, yes," she replied. "I'm fine."

"It's not the—"

"No, no, darling. I'm happy. That's all. I'm just too happy. I pray to God we can get that house. I pray to God we can. I'm just too happy, that's all. It's just too much to think that . . ."

They moved a week later and Larry found when he returned to his beat that his determination to have a home had had far-reaching effects. To his amazement, the people of the old neighborhood not only understood his desire to move but cheered his accomplishment and urged him on to higher goals. He was shocked to find that they considered him as something of a success symbol and wished all the best for him. It was a strange feeling for Larry to be so well known throughout the neighborhood. And since he had been placed in such an extremely high position in their minds, he found himself responding to it with a genuine concern for those who felt so much warmth for him. The children loved him, too, and he found that he had become the father image for a great many of them, even some of those who had fathers. The little ones tugged at his trousers and played cops and robbers with him, and sometimes, against his will, rode on the fender of the squad car until he chased them away in pretended anger.

One Saturday afternoon Larry stopped to play handball with some of the younger boys. The games were played across the street from the school store against the red brick wall of the school auditorium, directly under a sign that read NO HAND-BALL PLAYING ALLOWED. After the game a boy of about eight came up to Larry and said, "You know, Officer Atkins, it'd be great if you was a teacher, 'cause then you could tell us 'bout the war and all that, you know, and we could have some real honest-to-goodness fun in school, you know, and I bet you could teach us a lotta other things, too, you know, and I bet you you'd be a good teacher, too, and I bet you you could be principal, too, and . . ."

The idea seemed to explode inside his head and Larry thought about it for weeks, fighting it with every reasonable argument he could muster. Teaching little children? In grammar school? Maybe being a coach—but teaching English and arithmetic and spelling? Hell, I can hardly spell myself, he thought. It was impossible. He had just barely graduated from high school. How could he possibly become a teacher? But that's what he wanted to do. He knew now, after working with these boys and seeing their needs and the feeling of accomplishment that came over him when he had taught them something, that he wanted to teach children. He really wanted to teach. And they needed him. They needed him because he knew where they were weakest and they would respect him and they would either learn or else!

But all that was six years ago. That was when he and Beatrice were much younger. That was when they were not afraid to be dreamers and were determined enough to sacrifice and transform their dreams into actuality. That was when they were young enough to think that they could erase their past by beautifying the future. They never looked back, because behind them, they thought, was only sorrow and frustration. The dreams and dedication had been compromised away. From the very first compromise, they were over. The dreams and dedication were now thought of as only shades of the innocence of the time. That was all before he began to see the world with the cold, sick eyes of the materialist. The dreams were all before he had forgotten the reasons behind the seemingly uncalled-for actions of the people of his neighborhood. That was before the crime rate there took such a sharp turn upward, and before he had been shot while trying to break up a fight between a woman and a man. It was before he was knifed four times—the last time in the thigh, by a drunk, when he and John stopped at a tavern and walked right into a dozen knives.

John had become his partner only two years ago when the new superintendent had issued orders to integrate all aspects of the force, and when John joined him, Larry began to feel ashamed of these people he had known all his life. And in time he found himself disclaiming any attachment to the black world of perpetual crime. He found himself wanting to be something other than a black man and finally succeeded in convincing himself that he had nothing in common with these people except color, which was purely an accident of birth, so he owed them nothing. He would finish school and he would become a teacher, but not because he was dedicated, not any longer. They had killed his dedication. He would take up teaching because he wanted to break all ties with that animalistic world, and becoming a professional man would make the break final. This would put him at the very pinnacle of his middle-class society, and he would never look back again.

On Larry's tenth day in the hospital the orderly had wheeled him into the solarium, and he sat there in the sun, glad to be out of bed finally, leafing through picture magazines that all followed the same pattern (but now no one remembered which magazine had started the trend), and watching people in the parking lot two floors below coming and going. He could hear their heels striking the sidewalk. He could hear voices and the whistling of birds and the many variations of automobile engines firing up, and the whistling of people— almost always a light, happy tune and hardly ever in key. He listened to the sounds, sometimes with his eyes closed, and fitted to the sounds his own concept of the reality that should accompany and enhance them.

Then he heard a man singing and he knew instinctively that it was a black man. He knew it was a black man who was troubled, who was talking to himself and at the same time telling it to the world—telling, in his somewhat less intoxicated state than a few hours before, that he ached for one particular woman. Talking to himself and pridelessly singing it to the world in perhaps his own sad blues, he sang:

> Woke up this smo'nin', baby
> With my head just like it was befo'.
> Woke up this smo'nin', baby
> With my head just like it was befo'.
> Ain't got no chance to change now, baby,
> 'Cause you ain't with me, not no mo'.

Goddamn, Larry thought. Isn't there somewhere in this whole damn city where I can go without those bastards following me?

He opened his eyes and went on flipping the pages of the magazine, trying to ignore the singer. He hadn't noticed John Golich tiptoe in and was startled when he appeared beside him.

"What the hell are you practicing for," Larry said, "guerrilla warfare or something?"

"No. Thought you might be asleep and I didn't want to wake you up."

"Sleep! How'n the hell could you sleep in one of these steel monsters? And especially with all the noise from outside. Do you know that this little quiet room is the noisiest part of the hospital? And why anyone would have to build a parking lot right next to the hospital is beyond me. Brilliant damn architects never spent any time in a hospital so they don't know what it's like to sit here and listen to a hundred automobile engines start up." He made a motion with his right hand as if he had wanted to wave it in front of himself but remembered the pain that accompanied even the most minor movements and limited it to just a slight turning of the hand. "The hell with it," he said. "It's not important. You're checking out today, huh?"

John nodded.

"Great. You lucky bastard. Ought to be glad you're getting out of here." His lips were almost back to normal. The scabs from the tiny lacerations that covered his face had fallen off and were now replaced by shiny scar tissue. The bright scars were quite pronounced against the deep brown background of his round, almost boyish face. He changed his position often, moving slowly so as to minimize the pain. "I've still got those damn headaches, but I'd rather have 'em at home than here." He turned his head slowly, looked up at John, forced a smile, and said, "So how the hell do you feel, ole buddy?"

John smiled, wrinkling the massive discoloration that swept over his entire face like an acute perpetual blush. His ribs were still taped; and, like his partner, he moved with a certain amount of pain and ached in many places. "I feel like if I walk down the stairs slow I might be able to get to the car. And if I can get to the car, I'm a cinch to be able to take the ride home. And if I make it home, I'm going to sleep for two weeks."

Larry nodded his head. "Every time I doze off," he said, "some young thing who looks like she ought to be in high school comes along and sticks a thermometer in my mouth and says, 'Now don't go to sleep with that in your mouth,' and I always do. And if it's not that it's a needle in the ass or else blood—you know, every time I turn around they're drawing blood. I think it's a conspiracy, personally. They can't get blood donors, so they're stealing it from us. And so we won't know about it, they take a little at a time every morning. So get the hell out of here and go home where you can get some rest. There you'll only have to fight the kids."

"Don't worry. Mary's supposed to pick me up in about fifteen minutes. I figured I'd kill some time cheering you up. I'd much rather spend it with that cute little nurse, but she seems to have something against married men so I guess you'll have to do."

"Thanks. You're generous as hell. But that's not it. I predict it's only half-men she has something against. Now when you get yourself back into one piece, then you'll have a better chance."

"Hey, you really aren't so bad off after all," John said. "If I didn't know you better I'd swear you were smiling."

"Hurts too much to smile, but I fake it every once in a while just so the staff doesn't get too discouraged." Then his smile disappeared and his face turned into a cold, hating thing. "The real damage done to me can't be treated in this hospital, John. Nobody can do anything for that."

"Listen, Larry," John said. "The dicks talked to you the other day, didn't they?"

"You know damn well they talked to me. You were right there."

"No. I mean after that. I mean after I told them what I knew about the kid; about the possibility that it was, maybe—I don't know, maybe a mistake."

"Yeah, they came back and I told them I thought you must have been so shook up you weren't thinking straight. You don't want anything like that in a report, you idiot."

"But what do you think about it? And about the articles in the paper?"

"I don't think anything about it. You know as well as I do somebody always comes up with a story like that. It never fails. They give us those damn things; if we don't use them we're cowards, and if we do use them we're trigger-happy. Every time a cop shoots somebody they pour out of the cracks like roaches. To hell with them. I'm not running for office. I'm just doing my job the best way I know how. You want to know what I really think?" he said angrily. "As far as I'm concerned that's the man we were chasing. That's what our report says and that's the way it's going to read in everybody else's report and that's the way it's going to be. Case dismissed. Finished. Over with. No time to think about it, shit."

John lit a cigarette. "You want one?"

"Yeah."

He started to light another one.

"Don't light it for me," Larry said. "I'm not helpless. I'll light my own."

John handed him the cigarette and watched him struggle momentarily with the match. Then it was lit and Larry took a deep drag and stared angrily out the window at the healthy people below.

"But maybe," John said, "maybe this wasn't just any punk kid. Maybe he really was a good kid."

"Bullshit!" Larry said. "Like the good kids and the good, really good, good people who beat the hell out of us, huh?"

"No, not like them. That was different. That was a mob."

"Look, John, don't tell me about mobs. I know all about mobs and mob psychology."

"Yeah, but it still wasn't him. I had Mary dig up some back issues of the papers and he really was a hell of an athlete. You've got to admit that, Larry. And you've got to admit that it's a little hard to believe, with everything this kid had going for him, that he'd be breaking into a place for maybe a few nickels."

"I don't have to admit a damn thing. Listen, what about the doctor's son who's a junkie? And what about the rich kid who cut the little girl up into a hundred pieces? Not to mention the teacher who was going around enticing little boys to get into his car and then blowing the hell out of 'em. Good people, huh? *Yeah,* all good people. The world's full of good people. Like the good guy who finished making love to his wife and then reached into her, because she said she was leaving him and this was his last piece, and grabbed a handful and then pulled half her damn guts out. Remember that guy? He's the one that kept saying to me, 'Give me a break, buddy. Let me go. I'm white and I never did a mean thing to a Negro in my life.' Remember that? My great white brother. Crazy bastard. You gotta remember that one, John. I know you remember it. That was the one that made us both puke. And what did the guy—the good guy—say when we questioned him, huh? He said he just did it to save her from herself. She screamed all the way to the goddamn hospital. And sometimes, John, sometimes I can still hear her."

"C'mon, Larry," John said disgustedly. "You're taking this stuff too seriously. Look, I've seen enough of this crap without reliving it."

"Oh, no. You asked. Now I'm going to tell you." Larry's head began throbbing and he massaged his forehead with his palms. "He was an athlete, huh? A good guy? Friend of the people and all that shit. Well how many kids did this good guy put in the hospital in the past couple of years? How many gang fights has he been in on? Athlete, shit! He just never got caught before. You mention the word athlete and people start thinking about gods. What about all those baseball players who turned up owning slum property a couple of years ago? Some of the worst damn property in the city. They're not gods. People think they're gods because a bunch of fanatics yell their names and ask for autographs. Listen, I know better than you that a situation like we have out there can't deteriorate to that level without a lot of help—all negative—from the rich bastards. We get the shit kicked out of us by a bunch of bastards who live in their buildings, and everybody's touched. Their being touched doesn't stop us from aching. And what happens if we try to correct some of this shit, what happens if we arrest, say, just happen, accidentally, to catch one of those rich bastards speeding or something and we run him in? You know damn well what happens. We get read off by the judge right in open court in front of everybody like *we* were the criminals. We got one job, baby, and you better not forget it: We're hired to keep the goddamn savages chopping *each other* to pieces and see to it that they don't get out and start cutting up on the ones with money. White, black, green, yellow, orange—it's the same. It doesn't make any difference. The world's full of bastards just waiting for a chance to kick somebody's ass."

"Take it easy," John cautioned him. "You know you're not supposed to work yourself up like this. Your head'll split wide open."

"Who gives a damn? All that can happen is that I'll die. And that just might be a little better than this. I'm mad as hell, John. Maybe you're not because deep down inside you remember that you're white and you figured sooner or later it was going to happen to you—they were going to get even for everything somebody white had ever done to them. Maybe you feel like you paid your dues now and you're glad to have it over with, but I don't. I don't carry the guilt of the white race. I figure the only thing I've got coming from them is respect. That's *my* old neighborhood, John. I grew up two blocks from that street. And a lot of the bastards who worked me over have known me all my life. So what difference does it make whether we got the right man or not? You see what they think of us. They're animals! We take off our guns or turn our backs for a minute and they try their damnedest to kill us. Listen, Johnny, take my word for it—I know 'em—they really *are* animals— rotten. That place is another world, with all kinds of twisted rules, and if we weren't around to keep a hold on them, they'd be all over the city. That's what our job really is, you know, just keeping the animals all together and letting them chop each other up every Saturday night so they don't go around chopping the *decent* people up. Forget about the kid. He's not worth it. None of them are worth it. I know! I was part of that world, but I broke with it. I had my apprenticeship there and I stomped faces in and broke ribs and smoked my share of pot just like everybody else. I fucked in the alleys and damn near raped young broads under porches and broke my share of bottles over cats' heads and stole my share of cars and the rest of the crap. But I never got caught. That's the lucky part. And I came out of it. And there's a hell of a lot of them who could come out of it, too, if they wanted to, but they don't. They like living in that shit because they're so much a part of it. So as far as I'm concerned we got the right man. And if we didn't, if he wasn't the right man, that's just tough shit. It's just a sad mistake for him." Larry laughed and flinched from the pain. "That's one we won't have to arrest next year."

John put his hand on Larry's shoulder. "Give yourself a break, huh?"

"My own people, John," he said sadly. "My own people. But I don't belong to them any more. I don't belong anywhere to anybody."

John sighed. "Okay," he said. "I'll be back to see you next week."

"Yeah."

"Anything you want?"

"No. I just want to go home and you can't do a damn thing about that."

"Okay. I'll see you in a few days."

"Yeah."

■

They usually moved in at night. They usually moved after midnight when most of the neighborhood was asleep. They parked their cars in front of their new homes or backed their trailers into the driveways and unloaded them quickly and silently. Sometimes they were so frightened that they worked with a pistol or a shotgun nearby. They never moved all of their possessions. That would have taken too long. They moved only enough to be reasonably comfortable when things began to happen. Sometimes the entire family was on hand to unload the trailer, and sometimes the children were left with friends for fear that they might be injured should violence break out.

They moved the furniture in, pulled the shades, and didn't turn on any more lights than were absolutely necessary. The trailer was returned, the "for sale" sign uprooted, and then they waited for the next day when their white neighbors awakened and found the neighborhood integrated. This first night's sleep was always the best, because after they were discovered they would have to remain on constant watch for bricks and fire bombs and dynamite. And then, after enough damage had been done or after the man of the house had fired two rounds from his shotgun, the police would arrive and the crowd would be dispersed and a patrolman would be assigned to guard the house. Sometimes there would be people still living in the house and sometimes they would have gone to stay elsewhere until things quieted down and their presence was finally, resentfully, accepted.

Fire did not always break out, and dynamite was not always thrown, but windows were repeatedly broken and screaming insults chased them to sleep. Every week the glass man would come out and replace windows. Every morning the man of the house would grit his teeth and race the engine to drown out the insults.

At first the children were restricted to their own yard. Then finally, when they were about to give up, a white child would invite them into his yard. Then, perhaps in the same week, another white child would share their yard and then invite them to his. In time they would have reached maximum integration with more than half of the children on the block playing with them. And just when they had gotten used to each other, when black and white were finally adjusted and secure in each other's company, the panic would begin and signs would go up two blocks away, then one block away and finally in the block where the Negro family had moved. Real-estate agents would flood the neighborhood hounding people to sell now while the market was good and run off to the suburbs where they could be bled by other real-estate men.

The panic was on.

"Listen, Mr. Dulodrovic, I know this business. If you want to get your money out of this house you'd better clear out now while the market's hot. If you wait another year you just might end up living—well, you might end up living in a neighborhood full of niggers. Now I ain't got nothing against niggers, either, but think of your children. Look at that beautiful little blue-eyed girl you've got there. You don't want her—well, you know what I mean. How'd you like to have her come from high school one day a few years from now and tell you she's got a nigger boy friend. Now I'm not saying she would. I realize the kind of family background she's had here in this lovely home—what with the good religious background you and your wife have provided for her—but just think about that a minute and you'll see what I mean. Why, she wouldn't even know the difference. And besides that, Mr. Dulodrovic, if you sell now I can guarantee you that I'll get you eighteen five, but if you wait until all the other good houses on the block are gone, why, I can tell you right here and now that I won't be able to get you one penny more than sixteen. They've got the money and they're ready to buy right now. You know how they are; every one of them wants to be the first and if they can't be the first in the neighborhood, why, they don't want to move at all. The worst thing that can happen to you, sir, as I see it, is to be the last white man to sell. If that happens, you can forget selling this house. I don't mean to be cocky, Mr. Dulodrovic, but I don't think I'd even want to handle your house next year. I know no other reputable white real-estate agent would handle it, either. You might be able to get some of the Negro agents to handle it, but they'll steal you blind. You know how they are. No, sir—I don't want to tell you how to do business, because I can see you're a man who thinks for himself, but if I were you I'd sell and move on out west where all your friends are going.

"Incidentally, if you're going out to that new section we talked about the other day, I can promise you a good deal —one like you've never seen before. If you'd like, we can take a drive out there this weekend and look some of the places over. They're beauts."

Before long, moving vans are coming into the neighborhood every week, so that the children get to know some of the drivers by name. They no longer come at night because now there is no fear, there is no danger. Now the neighborhood is in transition and the Chicago school of integration is again following true to form. They didn't all want to move, but this thing they call Americanism takes guts to practice and they were gutless. This thing they call Americanism was only applicable when they were in the line to receive packages of food. This thing they call Americanism only worked when it was applied to someone else. This lie they call democracy, this insidious myth they call fair play, this vicious thing called the-American-way-of-life was not meant for the black man.

And rather than live with the black man, rather than live with their fellow Americans, they ran, and, without knowing it, without caring, they turned over another used section of the city to the black masses and at the same time increased their own burden with a heavier mortgage.

And now, every spring, somewhere in Chicago another Negro family loads their trailer and drives off to their new home where they will be the first black family on the block, and they are filled with anxiety, wondering what their reception will be, but knowing that no matter how much opposition they meet, they will not be turned away, they will live where they want to. They will not be turned away. They are often afraid, but they take strength in their fear and drive on. They usually move in at night.

■

The ride home was a quiet one. Mary had thought by the time John was ready to leave the hospital he would be showing some of his old comical ways again. She had hoped the glumness that came over him after the shooting would vanish as mysteriously as it had come, once he was on his way to recuperating, but she was wrong. He was a changed man now. "After all," she had said to herself one day after visiting him at the hospital and listening to him discuss the many problems that had suddenly come into his realm of vision, "I won't have to listen to the same joke a hundred times and laugh every time I hear it like I used to if he stops being so silly." But then she realized that she would miss her foolish husband who came home at least twice a week with a new joke and went from neighbor to neighbor telling it. She would miss the man who at every party could be counted on to entertain for at least two hours. To keep her spirits up, she told herself it was only a stage and in time he would be himself again and she would have the rest of her life to live with the funny man she loved and ignored most of the time.

At first she tried to be cheerful, telling him of the many amusing things their one-year-old son had done since he had last seen him, but she soon found that John was nodding and smiling only out of politeness, and was really not listening to her. She wanted to be quiet and share the silence with him, but she knew if she stopped talking she would think about his battered face and the scars from the sutures that seemed to cover his head completely and could still be seen although his hair had started to grow back. So to ward off the breakdown she kept talking. After a while John made no effort to be polite and openly ignored her.

His eyes peered forward but focused on nothing and his mind rambled back and forth over the years as he tried to remember what a Negro child looked like. He didn't know. He couldn't remember the few he had known in high school. They were just brown smudges. To him they were brown and had no character. They were people, but they were Negroes, and Negroes are brown and . . .

There were only a dozen or so there the year he entered high school, and it seemed to John now, as he tried to recall his first contact with that race, that all the racial difficulties had come and been settled before he arrived at the school. Yes, he remembered now, there were incidents, but they were only with a few Negroes—the ones who were hard to get along with; the ones who were not accepted by their own people. But even these he couldn't bring into mental focus. Wait a minute, he told himself, there must be some Negro I've met that I can remember. None. It was futile. Not even Larry—at least not before his face had been spotted with scar tissue—and he had worked with Larry for two years. Then finally one face came to mind and his lips turned up slightly in a smile.

Mary saw the new expression on his face, smiled, said two Our Fathers and three Hail Marys, sighed heavily, and then filled her lungs with pride at having been able to bring her husband out of his mood by simply being a woman; by being herself and sharing her feelings and experiences with him.

John could see the face more clearly now. He could see the hair, the eyes, the arms, the torso, the legs and feet and hands; such tiny hands—even for a girl. He searched his mind for a name, but none would come to match the petite young freshman with black hair (always short and curly), huge eyes, aquiline nose, heavy lashes and eyebrows. He could see all of her now as if she were standing on the hood of the car in miniature. She was about five one and must have weighed, he thought, about one hundred pounds. She was so black that when he first saw her he stared at her until she turned into the classroom out of his line of vision. She was so black and (now he was willing to admit it to himself) she was so beautiful that he could never take his eyes off her. Only now would he admit that she was beautiful. And only now would he admit that he, like every one of his buddies, had a crush on her. Sure, they were all crazy about her, he thought. Frank Sachs had finally gotten up enough nerve to ask her for a date and when she turned him down he was not so much angry as he was disappointed. But Frank didn't insult her like I did, John reminded himself. Goddamn, that was a long time ago and it's still nagging me. He was a senior at the time and working in the library during a free period. Football season was over and the library seemed as good a place as any for John to tell his jokes. She was taking a book out and John was going through the mechanics of stamping the date in the book and then on her card when he got the idea.

"Put your arm out," he said.

"What?" she replied.

"C'mon, put your hand down here."

She placed her hand and forearm on the counter, palm down. John spread his fingers open, placed his hands at right angles, then lowered them onto her tiny hand and forearm and said, "Let's play checkers." There was a line that day and everyone in the line saw what he had done and they laughed and their laughter warmed him and reassured him that he should be a comedian and go into the theater and stand on stages the world over hypnotizing audiences with his wit. But the girl didn't laugh. She just looked at him with her brown, penetrating, beautiful eyes and he could feel that she didn't hate him, but pitied him.

"Are you through with my book?" she asked in her gentle voice.

"Yeah."

She kept staring at him and it made him uncomfortable. She made him feel guilty for opening his mouth, for even thinking the joke. She made him feel guilty for wanting to ask her for a date and not admitting it to himself. She made him feel small and insignificant.

"Thank you," she said, taking the book and turning away.

"You're welcome, nigger," he said with a broad smile.

She never turned back. She held her head up, jerked her shoulders back slightly, pushing her firm, small breasts that much farther into her sweater and walked out like royalty.

"That was dumb as hell of me," John said out loud.

"What'd you say, dear?" Mary asked.

"Nothing." And he thought, what an ass. What a stupid ass. My kids won't do that. My kids'll know better. Why, they already play with Larry's kid and they see Larry and his wife at least once a month and we go to their place and they come to ours and, why, who knows, maybe in time they'll all grow up to be friends. And my boy won't have to make an ass of himself just because he's white and ain't too proud of it. She *was* beautiful, he assured himself. She was the most beautiful thing in the school, black or white. I wonder where she lives and if she's in Chicago somewhere raising a family or maybe she's even gone to New York and is doing something there. Huh, I bet she even went to college. Yeah, she went to college. I remember seeing one of the guys from the colored neighborhood after I first went on the force and he was telling me about this girl that was such a beauty—and that's the only one he could have meant. She was the queen at some Big Ten school or something. It's a funny world. He laughed to himself.

I called her a nigger and she went to college and I'm a cop. Sure is a funny world.

"We're home," Mary said.

John blinked his eyes and focused on the house to the left of the driveway. "I'll be damned. We sure are."

"Can I help you out?" she asked eagerly.

"No. Look," he stalled, searching his mind for an excuse to get away, "I'm out of cigarettes."

"We've got cigarettes inside, darling."

"Well, I want a cigar, then," he snapped.

Mary stared at him and a puzzled expression filled her plump face. This *was* a new John. In all their five years and nine months of married life she had never known him to lie so blatantly. Surely it was no more than the trauma he had experienced. Oh God, she thought, it couldn't be another woman. "John," she said softly, "we're home. Let's go in. The children are waiting for you. Don't go away."

"Mary, you don't understand. I'll be right back. It's just that the hospital and all the things that've happened have—"

Her face turned cold and she cut her eyes into him. "I went into a hospital just like that one five times, and every time I came home with another baby for you." The anger was mounting. The trauma of John's experience had burdened her, too, and she had reached her end. Seeing him on his way to recovery and knowing he didn't want to spend his first few minutes out of the hospital with her was unbearable, and all the anger of every old argument gushed out. "Do you know what it's like to give birth to a baby? Do you have any idea what a woman goes through to get the little bastards out? What kind of a man are you that you can't take a little pain without going to pieces? I gave you five children and never once complained about what it was doing to me. Look at me. My hips are so wide I almost have to have my dresses made special to fit over them. Oh, I know, exercise, exercise. You try exercising with a baby in each arm and one pulling at your dress. And I blame this on you, too! You're the one who could never wait when I told you it wasn't the time. I can tell you, John Golich, that three of those children I didn't want, but I had them because you couldn't wait another day or two. No, you had to have me right then and there even though I told you it was the wrong time of the month. You didn't care then, but you cared after I got pregnant and you care now more than you used to." She was approaching hysteria. "John Golich, if you've got another woman and I find out about it I'll . . . I'll . . . I'll divorce you—no matter what the church says. I'll divorce you and let you live in sin the rest of your life."

"I ain't got no other woman. I can't even handle you. God, that's all I'd need is another woman."

"Oh, you can't handle me, you say now. Well, that's a *nice* thing to say to your wife on your first day home from the hospital. That's a real *nice* thing for a husband to say to his wife." She clenched her fist and shook it at him and it shook with all the force of Ireland. "My father was right," she sputtered. "A Croatian is just another name for a Polak."

John was furious. "Your father was a dumb, drunken Mick and you know it. He wouldn't know the difference between an Englishman and a German."

"Ooooooh. The only thing that's different about you is that you're stupider than you were before you went in there. They knocked all the sense—what little there was—out of that dumb Croatian-Polak head of yours. Go on! Get out of here! See if I care! Go run after some other woman's skirts and see if I care." She flung the door open, got out, slammed it shut and shouted back into the car, "You know what you are? You're just a dumb cop. That's all you'll ever be is a dumb cop."

By now John had eased over to the driver's side, and he shouted back at her. "Yeah, well at least I'm not a dumb Irish cop."

She hunched her back, spun on her heels, and headed for the house, her plump, round body bouncing as she slammed her heels down on the sidewalk.

John didn't want it to end this way. Jesus, he thought, I'm not even in the house yet and we're fighting already. He leaned his head out the window and called, "Marilyn."

Mary heard him and couldn't help smiling, but she would not turn around.

He called again. "Marilyn, come back here and let's make up before I go. Marilyn."

She stopped. "I hate him. I hate him," she said under her breath. He could always do this to her, no matter how angry she was. And he seemed to know just when to say it to stop her from really doing something harmful to him. And no matter how angry she was with him or how much she hated him at the time, once he called her that name it conjured up a nostalgia that was reminiscent of their first year of marriage when she was so proud of her figure. Why, even after the first baby she had gone right back to normal. She had posed nude for him that day, and he had taken pictures, using up three rolls of film. While she was posing she kept saying to herself: If the nuns could see me now! John developed them in the darkroom —the makeshift darkroom in the closet of their first apartment. When the pictures were developed they compared them with the calendar, and John had made her feel so good that day. "The only difference I can see is that she's a blonde and you're a redhead," he said. How could she resist him?

She turned and shouted angrily, "What!"

"It's not that, honest, Marilyn."

She started back to the car, walking slowly, as if she expected to be spanked and wanted to prolong the confrontation. She stopped a few feet from the door. He reached out and touched her nose with his forefinger. "It's just not that at all,

Mary. You know me better than that. You know I'm not that kind of man."

"You're a man," she said, trying to retain some of the anger.

"No, Mary. It ain't that. It's just that . . . well, if I could . . . ah, hell, Mary, I never *killed* a man before."

Her face flashed to a sour white, freckles gone, sunburn gone, white, lifeless. "But, John," she said, speaking slowly, "it's not as if you did it all by yourself. Larry was with you and he shot too."

"No, Mary. It doesn't matter. Killing someone ain't easy. I killed him. We may have both shot, but as far as I'm concerned I killed him, and it's not a good feeling."

"Oh, darling," she said leaning over and kissing him. "I'm sorry. I should have known. Forgive me. I should have known. You want to be alone for a while. You're going to church."

He lied and took comfort in the fact that it was only a half-lie because he didn't answer and his silence was a resounding yes.

"I'll wait for you," she said. "Take as long as you want. I fixed corned beef and cabbage for you because I knew you'd want it. And I even fixed cornbread like Beatrice. It won't be as good as hers, but I got the recipe and I've made it a couple of times and the kids say it tastes just like hers, but I don't think so. You be the judge. Now go on to church so you can get back before I put the children to bed. They're so anxious to see you."

She kissed him again and he started the car, backed out of the driveway, and drove off. He passed the church, made the sign of the cross (thinking he'd better go to confession one of these days), and turned left onto the main artery that took him to the expressway, where he joined the continuous flow of speeders, peering ahead, to the side, in their rear-view mirrors for a blue-and-white police car, hoping to see it in time to slow down before the policeman clocked their speed. He drove for twenty minutes at speeds ranging from ten to fifteen miles over the speed limit of fifty-five; then he veered to the right, up the exit ramp, and slowed his car, sighing slightly as he always did when he left the expressway, surprised that he had been able to cover such a distance at such speed with so many cars passing and changing lanes without an accident.

He drove east ten blocks, turned left, and parked the car. He was only three blocks from the scene of the shooting. He wanted to prove something to himself. He didn't know why he suddenly felt the need, but he had to prove it. He had to prove that he was not prejudiced and that he would have shot the same way if he had been on a similar beat in a white neighborhood and the criminal had been white. He didn't really understand why he had suddenly come here. It was a compulsion. He was drawn, and would have been drawn even against his will, to this, the poorest and temporarily the most highly concentrated section of the sprawling, black south side of Chicago.

He got out of the car, started to lock it, remembered that if they wanted to steal it they would simply break the window, and left all the windows rolled down to give the impression that the owner was near and was perhaps keeping watch over his car, and began walking down the main thoroughfare. His bargain-basement summer suit was wet from perspiration and he took off the coat to be a little more comfortable on this hot day. The elevated train passed overhead quickly, bringing a fleeting shade but no change in temperature. Two boys walked by, smoking. He realized they were smoking marijuana, and instinctively he turned, sniffing at the air; but he remembered that he was not working and had no gun and no star. Besides, he said to himself, what the hell difference does it make. "Once a cop always a cop," he said, laughing at himself.

He stopped at a tavern and looked in the window at the people dancing in weird, uninhibited expressions of creativity, each movement smooth and original. He smiled at them and wished he could join them. He wished he could just once in his life step into a place like this and blend right into the crowd and be part of the happy, free, alive atmosphere these people created. The music screamed out of the juke box, the bass so heavy that it shook the windows, and it filled him with a yearning for a new experience, some new thing that would make him feel well again, some new thing that he had not had or at least had not understood before. He fixed his eyes on one of the girls dancing in the tavern. She was underage. No more than eighteen. She felt his eyes on her, and the eyes of all the other men in the room, and she reacted to their praise of her body and its rhythmic contortions with more controlled motion, more teasing, suggestive expressions. John stared at her until he realized that he had undressed her, carried her to bed, made animalistic love to her, and returned her to the tavern without moving from the spot.

"Whew," he said, turning away from the window and continuing down the street with the sound of the bass in his ears and the girl still imbedded in his mind. "That's another one, Father," he said out loud. "Maybe what I really need—no, no. Hell no. I got enough problems."

It was Saturday and there were many people on the street. John had always carried the impression of Negroes as being slow-moving creatures, shiftless and lethargic by nature. But today he was seeing differently. It seemed to him that they were moving much more rapidly than he had ever noticed in the past. And there was something else new, too: their grace. God, he thought, it's like a . . . like a . . . yeah, like a ballet. They just seem to glide along.

He began to notice the difference in walks, to which he had always been blind before. As many walks as there were people, but all with that smoothness about them. They were relaxed. They were relaxed and he wasn't. They made him nervous when he thought of his own stiffness. Granted, some of it was due to the injuries, but he could never move like these people. He could never be this free. Maybe it was because this was the forgotten section, the little animal den, the little crime corner that everyone had turned their backs on; the city officials, the civil rights workers, the do-gooders, even the churches, all, years before, had written this section off as lost, beyond restoration, and decided that with the next surge of urban renewal monies they would push for complete destruction of this neighborhood and rebuild it as something fit for human beings. These people knew they were the most rejected of all and in their rebellion they had found a kind of quiet freedom by ignoring the rest of the city and doing just what they wanted to.

John didn't know enough about law to fit the pieces together, but what he thought at this time was: How can we expect them to live by our laws while they're around us if they don't have to live by our laws when they're around each other and if we don't live by our laws as they affect them? They don't have anything, he thought, and yet, and yet they've got everything.

He walked on, passing taverns, store-front churches, jewelry stores, and restaurants, and stopped outside a barbecue shack. The smell of the barbecue was enticing to him, and he wanted some. For the first time in his life he really had an absolute craving for food. Larry and Beatrice had introduced him to their so-called "soul food," and he was trapped for life. He had to have some barbecue. He started into the store, but stopped momentarily to watch a half-dozen little boys and girls digging the dirt out from under the sidewalk just around the corner. He watched them for a while, wondering why they were not playing somewhere in a sandbox, until he remembered that the playground was several blocks from here. These children were too young to go by themselves; and because the adults were too busy, always too busy squeezing out a living, spending a great deal of time in frustration, burning up their energies in just surviving, the children would have to take their playground where they found it until they were old enough to race across the street between cars and on to the playground on their own.

He looked up the block. You know, he thought, if there was a little grass on those parkways it wouldn't be such a bad-looking street. But grass had to be maintained and that meant the landlords of these neglected buildings would have to employ someone on a permanent basis to do more than just empty the garbage and that meant cutting into their profits, so it was out. It also meant that children had to be disciplined and fences had to be built and maintained and a whole new way of life had to be taught to people whom nobody had ever wanted to teach anything to before.

"Yeah," he said out loud, "a little grass would change the whole damn neighborhood." And he marveled at his own wisdom. The thought that the only basic difference between this neighborhood and his and Larry's was that where he lived and where Larry lived there was grass.

Every now and then a child would stop digging, turn to face the cars traveling down the street, bright and shiny, and throw a pebble at a car the way the older children did.

"Jesus," he said under his breath. "The poor dirty little bastards." And he thought, But if their own people don't care for them . . . yeah, like Larry and a few others who talk about them even more than some whites do . . . Jesus, what chance is there for them except urban renewal and start all over again somewhere else?

John was puzzled. Why was he seeing so much today that he had never seen before? Why were they different? Why? His mind screamed at him. And then it came to him—the uniform. Of course. The uniform makes the difference. They don't relax when they see me in my uniform—me or Larry. They tighten up. Holy shit. I always thought they, maybe, sort of respected the uniform, but that's not it. They hate our guts. But here I am, a white man walking down their street, and no one says a word to me, no one tries to beat up on me or call the police—it's as if they didn't even see me. But with the uniform everything's changed. Now he remembered the two boys smoking marijuana. He would never have seen that if he had been in uniform. And the winos he had passed in the alley shooting dice. That all would have been different if he had been in uniform. He would have seen only the side he had seen for two years, the side they chose to show to the police; the other face of rigid control to be presented for all of officialdom so that they could preserve their freedom, their little taste of freedom within the framework of their isolated world that everyone in authority was waiting anxiously to tear down and build again.

John went back to the restaurant, stepped inside, choked on the smoke from the charcoal, and managed to cough out, "One order of large ends."

"Yes, sir," the girl said, sliding the glass door back and digging the long fork into a slab of ribs, rusty in color and adding their fragrance to the other scents of the little room, dark from smoke stains and dirty from lack of care. Unsanitary? Yes, but it was the way Larry had always told him, "Listen, the dirtier the place the better the ribs."

"You want hot or medium sauce?" she asked cordially.

"Hot. As hot as you can make it and then a little hotter."

"That's pretty hot, Mister," she cautioned.

"I know."

"It's your stomach," she said, dunking the short slab of ribs repeatedly into the open saucepan, and then removing them and laying them, dripping, on two pieces of bread placed on a paper plate. She tucked a paper cup of coleslaw underneath the ribs and slipped the plate into a brown bag. "I don't see how you can eat anything that hot," she said, handing him the bag.

"Does take some practice." He paid her, took the paper plate out, set it on top of the bag, and then scooped his huge hand under the bag. He tore off a rib with some difficulty and backed out the screen door into the street and continued on his way, eating barbecue and enjoying the hot sun as if he had been doing it every day of his life. He turned off the main street and moved his aching body slowly by the children. They stopped digging at his passing and longed for a taste of the richly seasoned pork.

John was enjoying the barbecue so much he didn't notice the children. He also didn't notice the one that had spotted him coming from across the street and darted to meet him, until he looked up and saw the child standing in his path as if daring him to proceed any farther.

"Gimmiesumribs," the little boy exhaled in an expressionless manner that, in the past, had always been offensive to John. It was another peculiar Negro characteristic he was understanding at last. The little boy had made a request in the only way he knew how; not begging, because rejection after one humbles oneself is indeed painful; not demanding, because demands of people in this weird world always brought about a reverse reaction or a counteracting force that led only to disagreement; but a statement—a blank, expressionless statement that could be taken any way you wished but that the speaker hoped would be taken the way he had intended.

John could never have put this into words, but he realized that this was all part of the Negro conditioning, all part of the ridiculous thing called life that has as many different meanings as there are minds to interpret.

"Gimmie sum ribs?" John mimicked him.

He nodded. "Yeah, gimmiesumribs."

John smiled. "Okay," he said. He stripped one rib from the slab and handed it to the child. The boy waited until John had withdrawn his hand before he permitted the emotion that was so well concealed to come gushing forth in one colossal, seven-year-old's ejaculation of a joyous, refreshing, uninhibited yell. "Yippie!" he shouted as he darted back across the street without looking to see if there were cars coming. When he reached the other curb he turned, the rib clamped firmly between his teeth, and said, "Sank you!"

John nodded his acceptance, began gnawing the meat off another rib, and continued walking.

Cute little guy, he thought. Looks just like Little Black Sambo. Hey! Those were good stories. That must have been it —my first contact with Negroes. No, it was before that. Must have been before that. Must have been when the Negro ladies would come into the neighborhood and do daywork for some of those ladies who could afford it. Yeah, but Sambo was the first contact with Negro children. "Goddamn it. That's rotten," he said out loud. There's a helluva lot more than you find in any Sambo story—a helluva lot more to people than you find in any one children's story. There should be books and books written about these people right here, he said to himself. But nobody talks about them. Nobody wants to see them. Why, what the hell, there should be a book written about this barbecue alone. This is not white barbecue. This is different. You can't buy this kind of sauce in a store. This is black barbecue— and he had to laugh at that because the last rib was slightly overdone.

A dog passed him, his nose glued to the ground, sniffing the history of the street for that day: No, he had not come this way yet today. Yes, there had been other dogs by, and there had been a rat, perhaps several, and a *cat* had come down this street, too. He raised his hind leg and added his statement to the history of the day at the base of a light pole.

John tossed the cleaned ribs in front of the dog which bit into the bones and began draining them of their last juices. When he had consumed them he raised his head and looked for the man who had befriended him. Not seeing him, he sniffed the air for the scent that had accompanied the bones, but his senses were not that keen. John had turned the corner and was now casually strolling past a vacant area that had once contained a row of six single-family dwellings.

The buildings, although handsome in design, had fallen into the category of slum property. They could have been saved, but there was an abundance of federal monies and the deals were made and everyone in authority was happy. The contractors could kick back to the white politicians and they would pass along only a small portion to the Negro ward committeeman because he had profited more by the increase in votes that would result from the huge public-housing building that would soon provide homes for two hundred families as opposed to only twenty-four originally.

And the city would ultimately profit, too, because the building would pay for itself (the politicians always said) and in time would bring in quite a bit of revenue. This was the whole principle of public housing as it had been applied in other areas of the city and it would soon be applied here in this forgotten section that could not be salvaged, only cleared away and made over in a way that could be better controlled.

John shook his head in disgust and moved into another block. Now he passed people sitting on porches, on steps, on curbs, in cars, boys on fenders. "What the fuck's that white cat doin' here?" John heard someone say. Then a voice answering, "He's probably one a them damn CORE people or somethin'. They always walkin' through here lookin' at us like we some kinda animals." "Yeah," said another voice, "I don't trust them cats, man. They some real twisted-around folks. They can't get along with their own people so they come around us and suppose' to be leadin' us somewhere. Better go on down South where they need 'em." "Ah, man," a deep voice joined in, "you people ain't never happy 'lessen you got somethin' to bitch about. They ain't all crazy. Some of 'em really mean it. I mean, after all, man, all white people ain't that way—they can't all be bastards. There's gotta be *some* good ones, don't there?"

The last sound John heard from this group was that of several voices joining in on the fun of an obvious answer when four or five people looked at each other quickly and answered simultaneously *"Sheet!"*

He could see off in the distance ahead of him two towering buildings side by side. Huh, he said to himself, more public housing for the people who can't help themselves because no one allows them to. But why did they have to make them all so big. Jesus, that way you get a concentration of people—and the word concentration kept coming back at him as if his mind had struck something of importance and fixed on it—concentration, concentration, concentration! He remembered when he had first heard it a few years earlier. It was on one of those discussion shows; an all-night thing. He had never been able to stay awake long enough to see the ending. Concentration. That was what they were supposed to do away with. He remembered the expert from the mayor's office saying—he remembered it almost verbatim: "One of the forces that contribute to vice and crime in our society is the high percentage of Negroes concentrated in an area that cannot accommodate them. This high concentration . . ." There it was. ". . . concentration of people will be eliminated when we build suitable structures and reshape the surrounding area to accommodate the people therein."

But it's a lie, his mind screamed at him. Let's see, they put up these damn things all the way from Twenty-second Street to Fifty-fifth Street—that's what, about—holy shit! That's four miles of 'em and a block over. No, it's only three miles. I.T.T. and a few businesses take up about a mile, but in one of those miles alone, on just one street, they must have seven to eight thousand families. Well, thousands, anyway.

His car was parked a half a block ahead of him. Thank God

it's still there, he said to himself. I couldn't walk much farther. Concentration, he thought. Why in the hell didn't I see this before. But how could the Negro politicians allow it. How could they allow it! C'mon, Johnny. Don't be so dumb. It's all one party, one force, one color after you reach a certain point. That's one place where things level off, anyway—all crooks together. That's what Larry meant. Concentration. Concentration camps. *God damn.* You've got to give it to those politicians— they're brilliant. Concentration camps without barbed wire, and a police force patrolling the outskirts so they don't break out and spread it over the city. It's a damn shame, too, because some of it ought to be spread over the city. Boy, if I could open a barbecue place in a white neighborhood and get some colored guy to cook, and get a couple of good-looking colored girls to work it like the ones back there, holy shit! I'd clean up.

John opened the car door, turned around slowly, lowered himself backward easily until he felt the top of the car hit his head and the seat the back of his thighs. He ducked his head and sat clumsily on the seat. He sighed, raised his right leg, then his left, and, bracing himself with the steering wheel, turned toward the front of the car. He grabbed the armrest and slammed the door shut. He sat staring out the window for several minutes at a bunch of boys playing softball in the street. Then he shook his head and started the engine. Concentration camps, he thought, goddamn concentration camps without barbed wire.

Part Three

■

The neighborhood was well represented by its unemployed residents. Inquests were public hearings so they could not be kept out, and the drama that would unfold, even though they knew what the outcome would be, was entertaining. It was a way of passing the time. So they got up early that morning and those with cars took some of those who had none. Others went by public transportation. They knew what the outcome would be but they wanted to be there to hear it and see how it would be done this time. They knew what the outcome would be, but they wanted to know what new method or weapons the white man would use on them this time. They knew what the outcome would be, but they were curious about who would sell out and how they would do it and to what extent they would go to further their own position and just how savagely they would attack their own people. They knew all of these things and they were prepared for them and they were angered by their treatment at the hands of the white man, but they would laugh about it that night, and they would laugh about the Deputy and they would laugh about the policemen. Still, they would remember it and they would nurture the memory because they knew their turn would come and things would be different. They were used to this way of life and didn't expect anyone, black or white, to be foolish enough to attempt to change it.

Before the inquest was over, those late-comers, added to the few who arrived early, had swelled the size of the audience to sixty people. There was hardly standing room, and when a baby began crying and had to be taken out, there was a great deal of commotion as people grumbled, resentful of giving up their positions at the show. It was a hot Chicago day, and the unwashed shirts and undergarments and the unpowdered bodies and the unscented heads, wet with perspiration, filled the room with new odors that cancelled out the arrival of a floater brought to the basement of the morgue from the lake only minutes before, and stood as a silent statement, as a badge of poverty, as the curse of rejection that these people carried with them wherever they went.

Sometimes they whispered softly, complaining about the heat, or making jokes about the funny little man at the desk whose glasses kept sliding down his nose. Some of them cursed the Deputy and the jurors and the police department, but so softly that the person standing next to them could not understand their whispering. Mentally they were all cursing the deputy and the six white jurors and the two white investigating police officers and the white and Negro patrolmen. Silently they were cursing the white mayor, and the white city council with its seven Negro aldermen, the mayor's black yes-men. And then, after they had cursed them all, they thought better of it and decided not to curse one white alderman from the University of Chicago area who stood alone among the other politicians in the city council as an exceptional white man who fought for Negroes. But all the others they cursed. They hated and cursed them, and some few people even prayed for their deaths.

They hated them because they were members of what was once called the honorable profession of politics; members who were seeing to it that the profession would not again be called honorable for many years to come. They hated the politicians they knew because these politicians swore an allegiance to

116

their party first, themselves second, and the people they were duly elected to represent last. They cursed these politicians because they felt the politicians wanted to keep the black masses not only ignorant, but also grouped tightly together, so that the whites who feared the blacks would not have an opportunity to live with them and discover their true worth, and thereby realize that whites and blacks were being pitted against one another. They cursed the politicians because they knew they were being sold from the auction block daily with such shrewdness that they could not prevent it. But they dreamed of a time when someone would lead them and bring the walls of the courts and the ceilings of police stations crumbling in on the contaminated whole of officialdom.

These people hated officialdom because officialdom meant a beating by policemen, followed by incarceration by a judge, followed by another beating by policemen. Officialdom to them meant the creation and enforcement of a double standard in almost every aspect of their lives. Officialdom to them meant the cry for their support every four years with campaign promises that no one expected to be kept because they never had been kept in the past. Officialdom meant public aid from agencies that had grown so strong that they could force the young adults to quit school and take jobs to support their parents and siblings. Officialdom meant the passage of laws to make credit easier with no laws to protect the buyers from the crafty manipulators of payment books. Officialdom meant white. Officialdom was white. Officialdom accepted only a few black people, and then made them over to think white.

Softly, crying silent, bitter, revengeful tears, they cursed and hated officialdom—they cursed and hated white!

■

Wilford arrived at the morgue early. The police officer met him and his mother in the lobby and ushered them quietly into the hearing room. They sat on the first bench and listened to the Deputy interrogate witnesses on a homicide case.

Wilford had been nervous and uneasy on the way over, slapping his thigh so much that his mother had told him to sit still and stop fidgeting. "Boy, you gonna wear that leg out one of these days," she said. The hearing room was practically empty, but the adult pressures were too much for Wilford, and he tightened up all over and began to experience a gnawing sensation in the stomach. His discomfort increased and he was beginning to feel nauseated when the Deputy asked the witness a question that relieved his tensions.

"When you saw J.B. take the gun out of his pocket, what did you do?"

"What did I do?" the witness said, twisting his face in disbelief. "I got the hell outta there. That's what I did. What you think I am, crazy? I did just what you woulda—I cut out." He clapped his hands one time. "I split."

The few people who were seated behind Wilford laughed and he joined in. And when he laughed he relaxed and the anxiety and fear left him and he was himself again.

The inquest ended and the room emptied and then began to fill up again for the next hearing—the room began to fill up with people who came to hear Cornbread's name avenged. Mr. and Mrs. Hamilton arrived with their lawyer and sat on the bench to the right of Wilford and his mother. Then the door opened and seemed to stay open for five minutes as a stream of people continued to file in. They filled the benches and then lined the walls and leaned their hands and heads against the walls, adding their marks to the many stains that had collected over the years.

Earl passed in front of Wilford, led by his father. "Hey, Wilford," he said, taking a seat to Wilford's left. His father sat to his left.

"Hey," Wilford said, rather coldly for him.

"How long you been here?"

"A long time. You had to come anyway, huh?"

Earl looked down at the floor and moved his feet back and forth. "Yeah," he said in a whisper. "my ole man's mad, man. He said he told 'em I didn't know nothin'." He lowered his voice and spoke directly into Wilford's ear. "He said I better not say nothin' or you know what'll happen."

Wilford turned and looked at Earl with gentle understanding. He thought: Man, I don't need no ole man if he's like that. My ole man wouldn't be like that. No, sir, not mine. My ole man would be right here just as proud as he could be and he wouldn'a let 'em talk to my mama like they did. My ole man woulda took that ole precinct captain and that funny-colored-eyed caseworker and even the police—he sure woulda—and he woulda let 'em have it. Bam! He smiled to himself about the vision his mind had just created. My ole man woulda said to all of 'em that I was gonna tell it and tell it like it is. He wouldn'a been like Earl's ole, sick ole man. Charlie ain't my ole man. Charlie ain't even my friend. Charlie ain't no different than Earl's ole man. Don't none of 'em care nothin' about Cornbread. My ole man woulda cared, though. He woulda been great.

The adult world had closed in on Wilford after the shooting. They had massed against him and he couldn't understand why. After he had told the older boys in the playground that he and Earl and Fred Jenkins had witnessed the shooting, the older boys had told other people and the word of what actually happened spread throughout the neighborhood as if whispers had been carried with the breezes from the lake. Within a week the entire neighborhood knew the truth. And even Mr. Smith, the white playground instructor, knew, but he had worked among these people enough years to know that he was not allowed the privilege of telling another white person. He was honored to have worked himself into a position of acceptance in the neighborhood and he could not jeopardize it by betraying a confidence. But he could tell it to a Negro, and he did. He went straight to the Hamiltons' house and told them what he had learned.

And the Hamiltons had gone to Mr. Jenkins and he told them he didn't know anything. Then they went to Earl's house and Earl's father had put them out. Finally they stopped Wilford in the playground and he was not afraid to talk and told them everything.

The precinct captain had heard, too, but he kept it to himself and didn't tell the alderman because it didn't seem important to him at the time. It became a matter of some consequence, however, when the alderman called him into the ward office and asked what he knew about the shooting. After they talked about the incident, he was ordered to see the mother of the child and tell her not to let Wilford testify.

"Oh, yeah," the precinct captain said. "I forgot to tell you. She's on aid. There's somethin' wrong with her heart or somethin'. I forgot to tell you that before."

"Great," the alderman said. "I'll find out who her caseworker is and get in touch with him just in case she tries to give you a hard time. The committeeman and me got a call from downtown on this thing and I don't want any slip-ups."

The precinct captain had indeed stopped off at Wilford's house and Mrs. Robinson was frightened, but not Charlie—Charlie was terrified! He was reduced to a stammering, obsequious clod. Charlie had gone to the playground to get Wilford. When they returned home he told Wilford to sit down and Wilford sat as still as his youth would allow him and watched the strange transformation take place in Charlie. He couldn't believe that he was seeing Charlie behave this way. He couldn't believe that Charlie was someone he had once thought could be his father. He couldn't believe that Charlie was so afraid.

"Yes, sir, Mr. Johnson," Charlie said, smiling and nodding his head rapidly. "If you tell us that's what you want, that's the way it's gonna be. He ain't gonna say nothin'." He turned to face Wilford and the smile was replaced by a cold, lifeless stare. "Boy, you ain't gonna say nothin' to nobody about this here thing. You understand? You hear me?"

Wilford was filled with the same rage that had become so much a part of his personality now. "You ain't my father," he said angrily. "You can't tell me nothin'."

Charlie jumped to his feet. "Boy, I'll beat your goddamn brains out you talk to me that way."

"Hold it. Hold it. Hold it," Mr. Johnson said. "That's no way to handle this. This is a smart kid. We gotta treat him like a man."

Wilford looked at the precinct captain and he thought, I don't need no help from you, you ole . . . you ole . . .

Mr. Johnson was dressed like his boss in blue summer suit, blue short-sleeved shirt and blue socks and tie and black shoes. He was short and muscular with a slight protrusion at the waistline. He was normally potato-brown, but was now tanned a deep rich brown because of the Saturday and Sunday afternoon softball games. His voice was high and piercing and he spoke so fast his words ran together, making it difficult to understand him.

"That's no way to treat my little friend." He looked at Wilford and smiled. Wilford turned his head away and saw his mother nervously trimming her nails with her teeth.

"Wilford, son, this is all something you don't understand, but if you don't say anything to anyone—and it's not like you would be tellin' a story—and do what we want you to do, I can promise you that we'll see to it that when you grow up you'll have a job with us and you'll be able to drive a Buick just as big as mine and wear clothes like this and all kinds of things. The alderman said to tell you that this is something you'll be doin' for your mother, too, because she needs all the help she can get. And he wants me to bring you over to meet him and let you look around the office and see how we operate. Won't be long before you'll be able to work around there summers while you're out of school, and you never can tell where you might go from there. Politics, son, that's the way to make it in this world, and we're going to take you in as soon as you're old enough. And we're going to take care of your mother, too, just like we've been doin', and you don't have to worry about anything because we keep our word."

Charlie nodded rapidly. "That's right. Y'all sure do."

"So you just do this . . . do what your mother tells you to, boy . . ."

Wilford thought. You ole funny-lookin' blue man. I don't like you, blue-man.

". . . and you'll be all right. I know you don't understand all this, but that's because you're so young. When you get older you'll understand why we have to keep our mouths shut real tight sometimes. This is all grown-up business and when you get to be a man, why, you'll know all about things like this.

Now can you keep your mouth shut like a man and do what your mother wants you to do?"

Wilford didn't answer.

"How about it, son?"

There was still no reply.

"Speak up, boy," Charlie demanded.

Wilford was trying to understand why it was so important for him not to say anything. It didn't make sense to him, because Cornbread didn't do anything to anybody; and he was already dead, so it wasn't like telling on him, and even if he wasn't dead, he still didn't do anything and they couldn't hurt him. He decided the only way to find out was to ask.

"Mr. Johnson."

"Yes, son."

"Why?"

Mr. Johnson was puzzled. "Why what, son?"

"Why don't y'all want me to tell the truth?"

"Oh," he smiled. "It's not that way at all, son. It's not that we don't want you to tell the truth. It's just that we don't want you to say anything just now. Now that's not tellin' a lie, is it?"

"Yes, it is," Wilford insisted.

"What? What? What did you say?" Mr. Johnson said nervously.

"Miss Carter said if you see somethin' wrong and you don't say nothin' about it, well, that's just the same as tellin' a story. That's what she said. She said"—and he pointed his finger at the precinct captain like his teacher did and tapped it against the air with each word—"if you know somebody else is tellin' a story and you don't say nothin' about it, well, then, that's the same as you tellin' a story right with 'em." He lowered his hand and sat up straight on the couch. "And I don't tell no stories, do I, Mama?"

"How old did you say you were, boy?"

"I'll be eleven next month."

"Well, you're too young to be talkin' like that. You better teach this boy some respect for adults."

Mrs. Robinson swelled with pride, and although she was still frightened, she managed to muster enough courage to come to the aid of her son. "Mr. Johnson," she said, her voice weak and giving out on her. She cleared her throat and tried again. "Mr. Johnson, I'll talk to him, but he's right. He's pretty headstrong and he's a good boy. He really don't tell no lies. And if he feels that what y'all want him to do is a lie, I'll just have to let him go on ahead and do what he wants to do."

"Wait a minute now," Charlie said. "Now you just stop right where you are and think for a minute. You know who you talkin' to? This ain't none of your women-folk friends. And on top of that he said they was gonna take the boy in there when he gets up some years. Now you just slow down and think what you sayin'." Charlie could not stand to be humiliated by both of them. He had to find some way to straighten things out to save face before the politician. "Mr. Johnson, you just go on now. I'll take care of all this. And I can promise you that the boy'll do what y'all want him to. He'll do what I tell him to do. Now you just go on . . ."

Wilford thought: Mama, you almost as good as my ole man would be. He smiled at his mother and suddenly he didn't mind all the times he had scrubbed the kitchen floor and washed windows and gone to the store and done without gym shoes and stayed home from the movies when Earl had money and he had none. He was amazed at his mother. He was proud to have been able to work for her. Yes, sir, he thought, Mama, you sure are gettin' to be a lot like my ole man woulda been.

". . . and I'll see to it that everythin's taken care of. You just leave it to me, Mr. Johnson, and I'll make sure everythin's all right."

"No, Charlie. No you won't," she said.

Charlie was crushed. "What?"

"Wilford's gonna do what he thinks is right and if he thinks it's right to tell what he knows, that's what he's gonna do." There. She had said it and she was shaking all over from the strain, but she had said it. She had gone against Charlie and the politician. Her son was not going to grow up that way. If she couldn't give him anything else, she would see to it that he would have his dignity.

Mr. Johnson straightened his tie and stood up. "Well," he said finally, "I can tell you one thing, you better make up your mind before your next check is due you."

She felt a sharp stabbing pain in the chest, and she gasped for air and then collected herself quickly. Oh Lawd, she thought, they wouldn't. They wouldn't. But she knew they would. "You mean it's *that* important that he doesn't tell anything?"

"It's *that* important," Mr. Johnson said. He opened the door and stepped out into the hall, leaving it open behind him. "You better make sure you know what you're doin'. If that boy says one word about this, you can forget about that welfare check from now on. You understand *that?*" He started down the stairs. When he reached the landing he called back to them. "You better make damn sure you know what you're doin'. You got an awful lot to lose."

The Deputy walked into the room, sat in his stuffed swivel chair, pushed his glasses back up, and began sorting papers.

Wilford elbowed Earl and whispered. "This cat's real funny, Earl. Watch his glasses." The Deputy moved his head and the glasses slid down. The boys snickered. "See what I mean," Wilford said.

Earl nodded. "Uh huh."

"He's real mean, too, but mostly he's just funny. He talks real funny, too. He's hard to understand. You gotta listen real careful sometimes. He fools around with them papers somethin' awful, and man, what he does to that pen . . ." He snickered. ". . . he just plays around with it all the time.

Earl laughed and Wilford elbowed him. "Be quiet, man. But ain't he funny? But, you know, Earl, he's mean, too. But don't worry, Earl, he can't hurt you. Besides, me and you can beat anybody in this room. Right?"

"Right." Earl pointed to O'Kelly. "Even that big cat over there."

Wilford looked at the officer, rows of flesh bulging over the sides of the chair. "Well," he said, "we may not be able to beat him, Earl, not this year, anyway, but I bet you we could beat him next year. Next year we can beat anybody."

"That's right," Earl said. "Just like we do the big boys. I'll tackle 'im and you hit 'im. Bam! Pow!"

"Yeah," Wilford said. "And we don't never start no fights, neither." He nudged Earl with his elbow. Earl leaned closer to him and Wilford whispered. "I think you gettin' taller."

Earl smiled and sat up straight.

Wilford nodded his head to convince him that he was serious and then they both looked at the Deputy and snickered again.

■

The Deputy cleared his throat. "Everybody here, Officer?" he asked.

"Yes, sir," O'Kelly answered. Today he wore a blue suit. It was newer and didn't shine as much as the suit he had worn to the last hearing.

"All right. This inquest will please come to order. This is the second hearing of an inquest into the death of Nathaniel Hamilton. Is there a member of the family present?"

"Yes, sir," Mr. Blackwell answered.

"And all of your witnesses are here today, Officer?"

"Yes, sir."

"And the policemen who did the shooting are also here, I presume?"

"That's right," O'Kelly said.

"Okay." He rearranged his papers. "Let's have a member of the family step forward to check out his family history."

Mr. Blackwell turned and motioned to Mrs. Hamilton. She stood, took a deep breath, and began walking to the front of the room. Her face was set, determined, oblivious to the crowd. She was a plain woman, wearing very little lipstick and no other make-up, and her hair had been hastily arranged. She was tall and bony and her lean face stood as an obvious statement of a life of torture, a life of struggling with all her capacity to provide food for five children. And it was strange that she should have to suffer so in a land that was said to be the richest in the world, in a land that to her did not mean prosperity, that meant struggling to exist, that meant going hungry so her children could be fed.

"Raise your right hand," the Deputy said.

She raised her hand and her facial muscles tightened at the thought of swearing to God.

"Sit down," he said brutally.

She occupied the witness chair and answered his questions without giving much thought to them. First her name and address, then Cornbread's; his date of birth; how long he had lived in the United States and in the City of Chicago; how far he had gone in school; her maiden name; Cornbread's father's name; the boy's social security number; his means of livelihood. To this last she answered "student," because that was the way the lawyer had instructed her to answer.

The Deputy said, "Well, he wasn't in school now, so he wasn't a student. He was just unemployed, right?"

Mr. Blackwell interrupted. "Mr. Coroner, he *was* a student. He was enrolled in college and was due to begin classes within two weeks of this incident. So you see, sir, he was still a student."

The Deputy was obviously angry that Mr. Blackwell had started disagreeing with him at the very beginning of this hearing. It was a little point, but he felt it was always better to have people unemployed in cases of this nature. It looked better in the records if it could be implied that he was a vagrant. "If he wasn't in school he wasn't a student," he said angrily.

Mr. Blackwell smiled. "Mr. Coroner," he said gently, "with all due respect to you and your office, you ask these questions of the family and the member of the family answers under oath. Now if you're not going to believe the witness, why not excuse her and write what you want to on the statistical sheet?" Then he smiled and the Deputy continued to flush with anger.

"All right. All right," he said. And he wrote "unemployed." Goddamn lawyers, he thought.

Mrs. Hamilton went on answering his questions, but now she began to rock slightly, so slightly that it was hardly noticeable. And she began humming as she rocked; between answers she hummed a sad tune that had no name. It was a tune she had hummed since she had been a little girl on the farm down in Alabama where they used to take her out of the colored school to make her harvest the white people's crops. She hummed the tune then because she was sad about leaving school. It wasn't much of a school, but it was a clean place to be all day and she never wanted to leave it, surely not to go work in the fields and get dirty and sweaty. She had always wanted to cry on those occasions, but if she had cried she would have been spanked; so she hummed her own sad tune and that way no one knew that she was really crying. It had become a way of life with her, and now she sat and rocked, answering questions about her oldest boy who had promised to buy her a house, and a freezer as tall as he was, stuffed with food. Now she sat and rocked and sang her song and no one in the room heard her except the court reporter, whose training made him aware of these little unimportant things that most people didn't notice. He was so distracted by the humming that he stopped writing shorthand and found himself behind, retaining two questions and answers in his mind. He gritted his teeth, jarred himself back to work, and caught up quickly. But all the time she was on the witness chair he listened to her humming, and it haunted him throughout the rest of the hearing.

Finally the Deputy said, "All right. That's all."

She rose and stood before everyone, a proud woman, a proud mother, without tears, without shame—a woman of dignity who would return home and go on rearing her children so they might have that special quality that would allow them not only to survive, but to prosper and give back to the world a substance it had tried to keep from them.

"Wait a minute," the Deputy said. "I don't suppose you got the twenty-seven dollars for the inquest fee, so you better sign this waiver."

She didn't answer him. She reached into her ancient pocket-book and extracted a twenty-dollar bill and a ten and placed them gently on his desk.

The Deputy was embarrassed. "Well," he said. "You don't have to pay it, not really."

"Thank you, Mr. Coroner," Blackwell said. "Mrs. Hamilton, why don't you sign the waiver?"

She shook her head in silent protest.

"All right," Mr. Blackwell said. "She wants to pay the fee, Mr. Coroner."

"That's crazy. I'm going to let her sign the waiver."

The lawyer shrugged his shoulders.

Her face was drawn and she shook her head in determination.

"All right," the Deputy said. He reached into his pocket and took out a roll of bills. Dumb bastards can't afford pride, he thought. Then he made out the receipt and handed it to her along with her change. And he wanted to say: It's not my fault it's a fee office. I can't help it if the state legislature won't abolish the fee. I know your son was shot. I know you weren't responsible and shouldn't have to pay the fee, but I can't help it. It's not my fault. "All right," he said. "That's all." He softened momentarily. "Thank you, Mrs. Hamilton. You can go back to your seat. And . . . ah . . . I'm sorry . . . ah . . . please accept . . . ah . . . our sorrow about your son's death."

"Thank you," she said. And she walked slowly back to the first row of benches and the audience was alive with whispers about her greatness; someone in the back of the room applauded, caught himself, and stopped almost before it was noticed. She sat down and stared again at the cheap rubber tile. Her husband reached over and took her hand when he noticed the tear working its way slowly down the left side of her face. She looked at him, smiled, and began humming her tune again.

"All right. Let's hear from the investigating officer."

Officer O'Kelly gripped the arms of his chair and pushed himself up, snapping the left arm like a twig, lost his balance, and righted himself in time to avoid any further embarrassment.

Oh Jesus, the Deputy thought.

Laughter could be heard coming from the back of the room.

O'Kelly looked at the Deputy, forced a smile, shrugged his shoulders, and stepped to the witness chair. Then he raised his right hand and the Deputy swore him in. Carefully, he sat down.

"What's your name?"

"Patrick O'Kelly. Patrick Francis O'Kelly, sir."

"You're a police officer from what area, Officer O'Kelly?"

"Area two homicide, sir."

"What's your star number?"

"One, six, four, eight, one."

"Wait a minute. Not so fast. Now what is it again, one—"

"One . . . six . . . four . . . eight . . . one."

Then the Deputy asked the time and date of the occurrence, the time and date of Cornbread's death. And the officer answered quickly, hoping to redeem himself and compensate for his clumsiness.

"All right. Tell us what your investigation shows in this matter."

And O'Kelly began, reading from his report, making the same grammatical errors he had made when he composed the masterpiece, and mispronouncing the same words he had misspelled for that reason. He went into some detail about what the police believed to be Cornbread's true background, and misrepresented the facts because that was the plan of his superiors and because he was secure under the protection of the coroner's office and because he thought there was no one to disprove that Cornbread was in fact the burglar. He shone as brightly as he could, filling the room loudly with his lower-class, back-of-the-yards imperfection.

Wilford had not understood everything the officer said, but he had understood the statement about Cornbread's alleged criminal activities and he was furious. He remembered the first time he had seen the officer. It was in his apartment and O'Kelly had come even before Wilford had wakened from sleep. He woke up and felt the heavy hand on his shoulder, heard his mother say, "I'll wake him," and looked up and saw the tall, wide man towering over him and seeming to fill the entire room. He was startled and thought at first that it was a gigantic leopard, but then he realized that it was only a white man, undoubtedly a policeman. He was not frightened, but he was slightly unnerved. He swung his legs off the couch and sat back looking way up at the red-haired man before him.

"Boy," O'Kelly seemed to shout. "What do you know about the Nathaniel Hamilton thing, or Cornbread or whatever you people call him?"

"What do I know, sir?"

"Yeah, what do you know? Did you see him the day he was shot?"

Wilford remembered the precinct captain and the words of warning of the older boys, and he said, "I don't understand, sir."

"Don't lie to me, boy. Did you see him!"

"Yes, sir."

"That's better. Now where was he? Did he come out of that alley? He did, didn't he? Ain't that where he came from?"

Wilford wanted to answer him, and his first thought was to

answer with a lie, to hide behind a Negro maneuver he had learned even before the age of ten; he wanted to hide behind the "I-don't-know-nothin'-sir" device he had known about ever since he could remember. But he didn't want to lie. His mother had told him that he must make up his own mind and he must stand on that decision; he didn't know what to do, though, now that the white man was there. He looked at his mother and saw the fear in her eyes and some of it was transmitted to him, and suddenly he was filled with so much terror that he was speechless and couldn't have answered either honestly or dishonestly.

Officer O'Kelly saw that the boy was trembling with fright and moved to intimidate him further. "You didn't see nothing, did you? You didn't see him at all, did you?" He shook him by the shoulders and Wilford thought his head would snap off.

His mother let out a scream and her fear vanished and turned to rage. "You take your hands off of him. Just who you think you are, pushing your way in here?"

"Shut up!" O'Kelly shouted.

"I will not shut up!"

And O'Kelly swung without even looking at her, striking her face with the back of his hand and knocking her into the wall. "I said shut up, goddammit! Any more out 'f you and I'll run the bot 'f you in." He turned back to Wilford. "You didn't see anything, right?"

Wilford had jumped to his feet and run past the officer, out the door, and over to Charlie's apartment.

The officer discovered he was talking to himself, thought for a moment, and realized that the boy had run out the door. "Come back here," he shouted as he hurried after him.

Wilford shut the door of the other apartment and ran to wake Charlie. O'Kelly followed him, kicking the door open. Wilford ran to Charlie's room and shook him. "Charlie! The police is beatin' Mama. Charlie, wake up!"

Charlie waked with a start and was on his feet before he realized that Wilford was in the room.

Wilford was crying now and the words came out so fast and so garbled that Charlie could not understand him. But he sensed there was danger, and he got down on his hands and knees quickly and searched among the boxes under his bed for his gun. Before he found it, O'Kelly stormed into the room, grabbed Wilford without even noticing Charlie on the floor, and pulled him out of the apartment and into the hallway.

Charlie took the gun out, released the safety, and caught them while they were still in the hallway. "That's far enough, man!" he shouted. "Just what the hell you think you doin', mothafucka! Who the fuck you think you are, you white sonofabitch!"

O'Kelly released Wilford and looked at Charlie as if he had never in his life known the meaning of fear and even now was incapable of it. "You better put that gun away, boy, before you get hurt."

"Are you *crazy*, you dumb white ass!" Charlie said in disbelief.

"I'm a policeman," he announced and assumed a superior stance.

"Oh," Charlie said. "I didn't know that." He began lowering the gun and he thought: Oh Lawd, they gonna take me to jail and they gonna beat my ass and I ain't never gonna get out.

"He beat up my mama!" Wilford shouted.

Charlie raised the gun again. Just then Mrs. Robinson came out of the apartment, her lips swollen and bleeding, and she headed straight for O'Kelly with a butcher knife in her hand. She walked slowly and deliberately toward the officer with her eyes fixed and her hand gripping the knife so tightly that her knuckles turned white.

"Don't cut him with no knife!" Charlie shouted.

She didn't hear him.

"Mama!" Wilford screamed.

She kept walking.

O'Kelly broke out in a sweat. He was trapped between an insane woman with a knife and an inexperienced man with a gun. He looked quickly for somewhere to hide. His eyes met Charlie's and they both glanced quickly at the stairway. Charlie motioned with the gun toward the stairway and O'Kelly broke for the stairs. As he passed, Charlie slammed the barrel of the gun down on the back of his head twice. O'Kelly ran on out the door, as if he hadn't noticed the blows, jumped into his squad car, and sped away.

"I gotta get outta here," Charlie said. "He'll be back and when they get through with me I won't be able to work for a month."

She nodded and hurried into his apartment and threw some things in a shopping bag. When she turned around, Charlie and Wilford were standing next to her.

"You better get outta here, too," Charlie said. "Get over to Hamilton's house and have him tell his lawyer about this. I don't know what he can do, but he might be able to do somethin'."

She nodded and started for her apartment.

"No, you ain't got no time. Come on with me. Inez can bring your stuff over. I'll get in touch with you over there and when it's okay I'll come back."

She agreed, and took Wilford's hand, and they all left by the back stairs.

When they reached the alley Charlie handed her his gun. "Hide this when you get over there. Tell that lawyer everything and tell 'im what that little shit's tryin' to do for them and tell 'im to get these white bastards offa my back. You hear?"

She nodded quickly, as if even Charlie had now frightened her.

"Goddamn shame. One little boy causin' me all this trouble."

She put her arm around Wilford's shoulder and he felt warm and less afraid. "It ain't his fault," she said softly.

"I don't give a damn whose fault it is. All he gotta do is what the man told him to do and don't say nothin'." He looked at Wilford and all the years of resentment mounted in his eyes. "You see how much trouble you causin', boy? You see how you fuckin' up everybody's life? Who the hell you think you are? If they catch me and work me over I'm comin' back and kickin' your little black ass for it."

Wilford hadn't seen Charlie since that angry parting. He wanted so much to be able to tell him that the lawyer had taken him and his mother to the police station that very day, and that after a conference with the captain he had sat in one of the tiny rooms while Officer O'Kelly interrogated him and could do no more than sit there angrily assaulting his typewriter with two fingers, preparing the statement exactly as Wilford gave it.

Wilford told him everything he knew, as Mr. Blackwell had suggested, and Officer O'Kelly, who didn't believe a word Wilford said, sat hunched over the typewriter, banging out his words and from time to time reaching up to touch the bandaged area, wet with blood, that was now beginning to cause pain. Wilford learned later that evening that Mr. Blackwell had made a deal with the captain. He would submit his client for a statement and the police would drop their charges against his mother and Charlie; otherwise Mr. Blackwell would see to it that a warrant was issued for the arrest of Officer O'Kelly for breaking and entering and assault. Wilford longed to see Charlie so he could tell him about the big bandage on the officer's head and the way he was so different when the lawyer was around.

■ "All right, Officer. That's all. You got any questions, Counsel?"

"Yes, sir, I have—with your indulgence." Mr. Blackwell stared at the officer for all of thirty seconds, and O'Kelly reacted just the way he had hoped. "Officer," he said, as O'Kelly's face began twitching, "I'd like to get the record straight on a few matters, if I may. You said your investigation disclosed that the decedent, Mr. Hamilton, was a member of a gang of some sort?"

"No. I didn't say that. I said I t'ought he was probably a member of a gang."

"Oh, I see. You thought that. Well, Officer"—he tilted his head and sighed, as if bored by the witness—"would you mind telling the Deputy Coroner and this jury and myself what evidence you have to this effect?"

"Sure. Well, we were . . . we feel that he was probably a member of a gang and it was this gang, see, that started the trouble afterwards, see."

"I realize that you believe this, Officer, but—I repeat—on what do you base this feeling?" He raised his voice and slammed his hand down on the table. "Just what shred of evidence do you have, Officer, that indicates that the decedent was a member of a gang?"

"Well . . . it's not something you can prove."

"You mean you're just pulling this out of the air? Is that what you mean, Officer?"

"No, no. I mean . . . it's the way things are out there . . . it's the way it's been . . . we just think it. That's all, we just think it."

"It would behoove you, Officer, to think less and know more."

"All right," the Deputy said. "Don't argue with the witness, Counsel. He's answered your question. Now don't argue with him."

"I beg your pardon, Mr. Coroner, but the witness is not being responsive."

"All right. All right. Get on with it."

"Yes, sir." He flipped through his notes. "Now as I understand your testimony, the two police officers seated behind you were chasing someone—that is, Officers Golich and Atkins— were in pursuit of someone they believed to be a burglar. Is that correct so far, Officer?"

"Yes, sir."

"Fine. We got that answered. And they pursued this person through an alley and lost sight of him for a split second as he turned out of the alley. Is that correct? Do I understand your testimony correctly so far?"

"Just a split second."

"Yes, I understand that. Just as long as it would take to blink one's eye, perhaps?"

"Yeah, I guess that's all it took."

"All right. And then they proceeded one block—in this split second, of course—and turned the corner and saw the decedent and fired at him; is that correct?"

"No, no. There's more to it than that, Counsel. They told him to halt, see. They told him to halt first, see. And they t'ought it was a gun and they fired at him."

"Oh, I see. They told him to halt and they shot four times

and killed him. And did they do this in the same kind of split second that they traveled a block, or was this really done in a longer time than that split second that is really no more time than the batting of an eye?"

"They told him to halt and they t'ought he had a gun and they fired at him then, see."

"Oh, yes. That's right. I forgot about the shiny object. What kind of a day was this, Officer O'Kelly?"

"Rain."

"It was a rainy day; is that correct?"

"Yeah, rainy day. Rained all day. Rained all day and all night too." He was perspiring heavily. He reached into his pocket and took out a handkerchief. He opened the handkerchief and began mopping his forehead and the back of his neck.

"It rained all day, you say. And would that mean that it was an overcast day?"

"Yeah."

"I see. And that means, I would assume, that there was no sunlight—at least there were no rays of sun—not the kind of bright day you have when it's not raining, surely?"

"Yeah. A dull day."

"Overcast day. It was a heavy rain, wasn't it?"

"Yeah. Bad rain."

"And that would mean that it was pretty dark, wouldn't it?"

"Sure it would."

"I see." He nodded his head and wondered if he should ask how anything reflected light on a heavily overcast day. He decided to go all the way. "Officer, have you ever seen anything reflect light on an overcast day?"

"Huh?"

"All right, now just a minute," the Deputy said, realizing that the officer was trapped and that he must intercede to save him. "I've told you time and again, Counsel, not to argue with the witness and I'm not going to let you go on like this. Besides, you know there's no cross-examination permitted at a coroner's inquest. Just ask him direct questions and he'll answer them. And if he can't answer them he'll say so."

"Yes, sir, Mr. Coroner." And he thought, Well, you saved him that time. But there's still another way. "May I continue, Mr. Coroner?"

"Yes. But let's not take all day. We've got a room full of witnesses that you brought in to testify."

"That the police officer brought in, sir. These are not my witnesses. These are witnesses for the Coroner."

"All right. All right."

"Officer, did you ever find the so-called weapon that the decedent was alleged to have had in his possession?"

"No."

"Is it possible that he didn't have a gun or a weapon at all, Officer?"

"As far as I'm concerned, he did. I think he did."

"I didn't ask you what you thought, Officer. Were you there at the time of this occurrence?"

"No, sir."

"So you don't know of your own personal knowledge that he did have a weapon, do you?"

"No."

"All right. Now, did you find a weapon on the scene?"

"No."

"And did anyone tell you they definitely saw a gun?"

"The officers said they t'ought he had a gun in his hand."

"Did anyone tell you—I repeat—that they definitely saw a weapon in his hand at the time of this occurrence?"

"No, sir."

"And isn't it true that one of the witnesses did in fact tell you that the decedent had in his possession at the time of this murder—"

"Now just a minute—"

"—a bottle of orange pop?"

"Counsel. You're leading the witness. Don't lead the witness. Just ask him direct questions."

"All right, Mr. Coroner. Did a witness tell you what the decedent had in his hand at the time of this shooting, Officer?"

"A witness said something, yeah. But I don't believe that, either."

"You're awfully opinionated for an impartial investigator. I assume it is your function to be impartial. And you were not on the scene; is that right?"

"No."

"Well, how can you form such solid convictions about what actually happened there when you weren't there?"

"My investigation."

"Very good. And from your investigation, did a witness tell you what the decedent had in his hand?"

"Yeah, he said what he t'ought he had."

"No, no, Officer O'Kelly. Did he *tell* you what he *knew* he had in his hand?"

The officer unbuttoned his coat and now mopped his face as well as his forehead and neck. "He said he had a pop bottle in his hand," he said angrily.

"A *pop* bottle? Is that what he said?"

"Yes!"

"It was a bottle of orange pop, wasn't it, Officer?"

"I don't remember what flavor, Counsel."

"Well, would you like to check your report to refresh your recollection? I'd like you to be positive. After all, this is a serious matter."

"If you say it was orange pop, it was orange pop."

"No, no, Officer. I want you to say. I'm not under oath, but you are. So you tell me what *you* found it to be."

"Oh, for God's sake," the Deputy growled. "What was it? If you know, Counsel, go ahead and say what it was."

"I know, Mr. Coroner, but the officer has it in his report and I want him to refresh his recollection."

O'Kelly glanced quickly at his papers and then back to Mr. Blackwell. "It was orange pop, a bottle of orange pop."

"That's right, Officer, it was orange pop. And where did the witness say the decedent had been prior to going out onto the street on this rainy day with the bottle of orange pop in his hand?"

"He said he had been in the store."

"In the school store across the street from the school; is that the location he was at?"

"Yeah."

"And what did the witness say he was doing in the store, Officer?"

"He had a bottle of pop."

"I see. Now was that the same bottle he had in his hand when he was running down the street and was shot in the back?"

"No, it was another bottle."

"Oh, I see. Then he had two bottles of pop; one he drank in the store and the other one he took with him when he left the store. Now is that correct, Officer? Is that what the witness told you when you took the statement from him at the police station?"

"You know what he told me, Counsel," he said angrily. "You was there with me and you heard every word he said at the time. You brought him in."

"That's right, I did, Officer."

"You took the witness to the station?" the Deputy asked.

"That's right, I did, Mr. Coroner."

"Then he is your witness if you took him there."

"No, that's not right, Mr. Coroner. I took him there because the officer had been to the home of the witness earlier that day and there was some difficulty there. The witness, who is a ten-year-old child, was afraid to talk to the officer at that time. As a result, his mother brought him to me and requested that I accompany her and her son to the police station. Officer O'Kelly knew about the witness and had been there trying to interrogate him."

"Oh," the Deputy said. "Okay. Okay. Go ahead, Counsel. Let's get this case over with."

Mr. Blackwell paused for a moment to find his place and pick up the pattern he was developing. His eyes sparkled, and he spoke quickly. "How long does it take to drink a bottle of pop, Officer?"

"I don't know."

"Well, how long do you think it would take?"

"Couple minutes."

"A couple of minutes?"

"Well, maybe a few minutes. I don't know."

"Would you say five minutes, four minutes, ten minutes?"

"It wouldn't take ten minutes. Not for him. These kids drink that stuff in a couple minutes."

"And would you say it was more like three minutes, maybe?"

"About that."

"And three minutes is longer than a split second; isn't it?"

"Yeah."

"And you say the officers that were in pursuit of the burglar only lost sight of him for a split second; is that correct?"

"That's right."

"Officer, do you have the so-called gun, the bottle of pop in the hearing room today?"

"No, sir."

"Why not? What happened to it? Did you see it when you arrived on the scene?"

"I don't know what happened to it."

"How long after this occurrence did you arrive on the scene, Officer?"

"About ten minutes."

"Were you one of the officers who was called out to break up this disturbance that began after my client's son was murdered?"

"I was called out, yes."

"And did you see the pop bottle when you arrived on the scene?"

"No, I wasn't . . . I don't know . . . it was . . . everything was in the street, and there were people everywhere."

"And you say the patrolmen told him to halt?"

"Yes."

"Did they announce their office?"

"Yes. They said, 'Halt. Police.' "

"And what did the witness tell you?"

"The witness didn't say anything about that."

"Didn't the witness tell you, Officer, that they began firing as soon as they got out of their squad car?"

He loosened his tie. "Well, I'm not sure what he said."

"Would you like to refresh your recollection? You may if you wish. I'm sure you have his statement with you, don't you?"

"I don't think I have."

"Oh, come now, Officer O'Kelly, surely you wouldn't leave the statement of the most important witness at the police station. You do have the statement somewhere, either in your possession or at the station, don't you?"

"I can't find it in my records. I looked for it before I came here." He unbuttoned his shirt. The collar was gray from perspiration. "I looked for it for twenty minutes."

"Well, Officer, you do have other copies, don't you?"

"Yes, downtown. They keep all the copies downtown."

Mr. Blackwell dropped his pencil. "Mr. Coroner," he said disgustedly, "this is inexcusable. In all my years as a lawyer I have never in my life seen this kind of flagrant abuse. This is indeed an offense that amounts to criminal negligence. Surely the Coroner will reprimand the officer for coming to this hearing and not being prepared. What are they trying to *hide*, Mr. Coroner?"

"Well, Counsel, if the statement's been lost it's just been lost. He said they have another copy downtown. And since the witness is here, he can testify and tell his story to this jury. I realize it is somewhat of an imposition, but since the witness is here, there's no real harm done."

"For all the good the investigating officer has been in this case with his sloppy investigation, he could have lost himself! It's hard for me to believe that in the City of Chicago *today* this kind of abuse still exists. What are we doing, Mr. Coroner, slipping back to the dark ages?"

"Counsel, please. Don't lose your temper."

"I'm not losing my temper, Mr. Coroner, but I am disturbed. Not only is he a liar, but he's not even smart enough to do it with a little finesse. He leaves the statement of the most important witness and then comes in and tells us that he doesn't know what the witness said."

The Deputy shrugged his shoulders. He's a real fighter, he thought. Putting on a good show for his client. "The only thing I can suggest that we do, Counsel, is continue the case. But with all these people here, I hesitate to do a thing like that."

"I see no reason for inconveniencing all these people, either, Mr. Coroner. But it's pretty obvious to me what the police department is trying to do in this case, and I want the record to show at this time that I *have* called the police officer a liar."

O'Kelly flinched, gritted his teeth, but made no comment.

Mr. Blackwell made a sweeping motion with his hand. "That's all. I don't want to waste my time with a liar. I don't have any further questions."

"Okay," the Deputy said. "That's all, Officer. You can go back to your seat."

O'Kelly got to his feet.

"Let's have your first witness."

"Fred Jenkins is our first witness, sir." O'Kelly went back to his chair against the wall and sat down next to Officer Golich.

■

The city had changed. The expansion of the trucking industry and the decline of railroading had shot the need for one massive butchery. The increasing taxes and high cost of labor had forced the packing industry to decentralize, to take their businesses and scatter them throughout the country where the labor market was full and unions were less powerful and municipalities offered special, guaranteed tax reductions. And when the stock yards blew up and disintegrated in the faces of the people of Chicago, thousands of these people were left unemployed. And other industries, feeling the noose of taxation and the cries of stockholders, followed the great meat packers throughout the country. And thousands more were out of work and the newcomers to the city were met with long lines at the state employment offices, long lines of black people whose cards were marked with a special code so the processors would know from the cards whether or not they were Negroes and would not send them to the offices that wanted whites only.

The city had changed. The city became, rather than a city of workers turning back into circulation the goods of their labor, a welfare city. It became a city of social workers looking down their noses at the helpless thousands they detested. The black City of Chicago, mysteriously thriving within the confines of its limited opportunity, became a city of roamers. To be gainfully employed was to be exceptional. To prepare for the future was pointless because everyone knew there were no jobs to be had—not for them.

The city had indeed changed. The great city that had provided jobs for its residents for so long now provided jobs for those countless thousands who lived ten and twenty and as far as fifty miles from its nucleus. The rich suburbs were made richer by the ailing Chicago, and its black residents, occupying almost half of its territory, were made more dependent.

Some said the welfare city was planned by politicians. They said it was one way of assuring continued dominance over the masses. Others said it was an accident, a freak thing that would be corrected in time. "It takes time," they said. And there were those few who said it was all because of the inability of the black man to adjust to urban living.

And some few knew that it was because of the kind of economic slavery the whites had forced on the blacks and that it had reached the end of its cycle and that the whites were losing control and were frightened and insecure because the world was now looking at this working democracy and they would soon have to put the spoken and written word into practical application. They knew a revolution had begun and Chicago was due for greater changes that would destroy the old inadequate ways and force the city to recognize one-third of its population and let them develop freely or else die itself as the price for holding them down.

■

Mr. Jenkins worked his way through the crowd. Once he cleared them he straightened his hunched back for the first time in months, shoulders squared, head high, eyes darting over the front of the room, and walked the long, lonely path to the witness stand. Lately he had taken to leaving his store in the early afternoon hours and going to the beach where he lay in the sand and admired the young girls and young mothers, like the other males collected there. He delighted in the firmness of young girls, their upright, almost hard breasts and piercing nipples that bored into his mind and sent him home every day a little closer to the act of seduction that he would perform before long. Before winter he would have his young girl or girls, and recapture a bit of his youth.

In the past he had settled for occasional affairs with mature women; but their demands were too great. They wanted too much; too much money, or too much time, or too much of him. They made him work too hard for them and he had begun to feel insecure. His manhood was in danger, and he had resolved to go after someone younger and less experienced; someone that would give his ego a boost and make him a man again. At first he had stayed in the shade, not wanting to tan and look like all the other people in his world. This was an asset, he felt, his absence of color, and he didn't want to become just another black man. But one day he fell asleep, and the shade moved beyond him, and when he woke up an hour later he was burned. When his skin peeled, the whiteness was gone and his gray hair was more pronounced. He had become handsome. The next day a young girl knelt in the sand, ran her hand over his forehead, and said, "Mr. Jenkins, for an old cat you sure look sharp now that you got some color." After this he sat in the sun and grew browner and prouder and cockier with each day.

And now, sitting in the witness chair, he was tanned and peeling and he felt handsome. He felt reckless and wanted to live again. It was as if he had been dead for years and had learned only lately how uncertain life really is. As if Cornbread's death and the events that followed had awakened in him the knowledge of his own approaching end, and he wanted to reach out and taste all that he could of life before it was ended and he became another cold, forgotten thing like the people in the basement of the morgue.

He was sworn in and the Deputy began interrogating him. Name, address, occupation.

Wilford nudged Earl. "You watch Mr. Fred," he whispered. "You hear me? You just watch Mr. Fred tell 'em." Then to himself: Go on, Mr. Fred. The joy of the pending revelation thrilled him and his face was a round, beaming smile. Hot dog, he said to himself. You tell 'em, Mr. Fred. I'm with you, Mr. Fred. Sic 'em. Get 'em. Go on—let 'em have it! He remembered the day in the store when he had sought advice from Mr. Jenkins. Wisdom had flowed from Mr. Jenkins' lips and Wilford had finally seen why the older boys liked him. He had even gotten off his stool and come around to the other side of the counter, put his arm around Wilford's shoulder and spoken to him man-to-man.

"Listen, Will," he had said in a fatherly way, "a man's gotta do what he thinks is right. Ain't no way in the world you can call yourself a man and not do what you *know* to be right. So if nobody else does it, Will, you and me—we'll tell 'em. You and me, Will—we'll let 'em have it. And if they don't like what we got t' say—that's just tough shit, Will. That boy was just like my own son. I'd like to see 'em try to stop you and me from talkin'. I'd like to see 'em try to stop us from tellin' it like it is. They'll have to *kill* me first. But you don't do what I do, Will, just because I'm doing it. You do what you think is right. You gotta live with yourself. No matter how long you live, you always gotta live with yourself. You understand that? Sure you do. So you do what you know is right and that way you can sleep nights. That way you'll always be a man, son."

"What do you know about this occurrence?" the Deputy asked. "What do you know about this robbery or this shooting, or both?"

"I don't know nothin'," he said coldly.

Wilford shut off his smile and stared at Mr. Jenkins in disbelief. "Oooooo, Mr. Fred," he whispered. "Oooooo, Mr. Fred, you *lie*." He looked at Earl and shook his head. Earl shrugged his shoulders. He turned back to the store owner. "That's *wrong*, Mr. Fred," he said loud enough so his mother could hear him. She touched his knee and said, "Quiet, Wilford." And he thought: Man, you sure are a wrong-doin' cat. And after all that stuff you told me, too, and after sayin' how we was gonna do so much—you and me—and after makin' me go on and do what I done and makin' my mama get kicked off of aid and makin' Charlie run away and makin' me go on up there to the police and say it like I did and—oooooo, you *lie*.

Mr. Blackwell wrote on his note pad: "One down. Two to go. Hail glorious democracy." You rotten yellow bastard, he thought.

"So you didn't see this," the Deputy said.

"No, I didn't see it. How could I? I got things to do in my store. I ain't got time to sit around lookin' out the window all day."

The Deputy was warmed by his response. He felt secure

enough to pursue other avenues and tighten the case for the officers. "All right, now I heard from the investigating officer before this hearing began that some witness had said that this decedent was in your store before the shooting. Is there any truth to that?"

"Who, Cornbread?"

"The decedent—this boy—Hamilton?"

"No, he wasn't in my store. Wasn't nobody in my store."

"Well, if you didn't see anything, did you hear the shots?"

"Shots? How'm I gonna hear shots when it's lightnin' and thunderin' out there like it was?"

The audience was silent. The proprietor had lived up to their expectations. They despised him for being what he was, but they knew he had to answer the way he did. He had no choice. In time they would forgive him, but they would never forgive the butchers who cut out his soul and left him one of the lifeless. They didn't know what means officialdom had gone to to silence Mr. Jenkins, but they knew he had not turned on his people of his own volition. They knew some extension of the white Chicago had entered his world and made him join the ranks of the butchers. They had lost another soul-brother and they were sad that he had left them because they knew he would never belong to their world again, but would now be suspended between the black and white worlds; alone, not even belonging to the thousands of others who had sold out (because there could be no unity among traitors who distrusted one another), not belonging anywhere, but remaining foreign to all groups from this day on.

"So when's the first time you knew about this occurrence?"

"First time I knew anything was when they started throwin' all that crap through the windows. I was movin' some pop up —bringin' the cases up front from the back of the store—and the next thing I knew, they started throwin' all kinds of crap through the windows and I ran to the back of the store to get my gun and before I could get it and get back, the police were chasin' people through my store." He told his story as if he were reading a prepared statement with no emotion. He spoke in a slow, deliberate monotone that pleased the court reporter, who was sometimes disturbed by Negro witnesses because they spoke rapidly and were difficult to understand. "They ran through my store like it was an expressway."

Laughter filled the room and the Deputy and Mr. Jenkins smiled.

Mr. and Mrs. Hamilton looked at each other and shook their heads. Then they both looked at Earl and Wilford. The boys lowered their eyes and moved their feet nervously on the floor.

Then Wilford stared at Mr. Jenkins, searching his face for some sign of a scar or a bruise. Finding none, he concluded that they must have tortured him somewhere else. Yeah, his mind told him, I bet they kicked him down there and hit him in the stomach with those things they got and I bet they even *stood* on him and one of 'em held his arms behind his back like they do in the movies and television and the other one beat him up real good. He looked at Mr. Jenkins' hands, resting in front of him on the table, his long fingernails cleaned and well groomed. Yeah, I bet they stuck knives in his fingers and . . . and . . . ooooo, Mr. Fred, they must 'f beat you up real good, 'cause you *lie.*

Two plainclothesmen had in fact visited Mr. Jenkins, but they had not laid a hand on him. They were old-timers on the force and they knew their profession well; they knew subtle ways of intimidation and were not as crude as Officer O'Kelly. They entered the store and flashed their badges.

"Police," the dark-haired one said.

"Okay," Mr. Jenkins answered. "What's up?"

The heavier, gray-haired one straddled a stool. "Did you see the shooting the other day?"

"Yeah," Mr. Jenkins said arrogantly, "I saw your boys gun

that kid down. You guys gonna get 'em for it, or are you gonna just let it go as another accident?"

The dark one took a seat beside his partner. "You did see it, huh? That's strange. How could you see it when you were busy? Give us a couple of bottles of pop."

Mr. Jenkins swung around to the ice chest. "What kind?" he said.

"Marijuana," the gray one said.

He swung back around, "Listen," he said. "I got things to—" And his eyes fell on twelve reefers that the gray officer was placing in an even straight line. "Don't you sell marijuana here, too? I thought all you colored store owners had a supply of marijuana for the school kids."

"Yeah," his partner said. "I hear from some of the stoolies in the neighborhood that that's all these kids do around here. You know, when the papers hear about this—" He whistled. "Selling reefers to *grammar* school kids. When the judge gets through with— What did you say about the shooting?"

Mr. Jenkins chuckled slightly. "Fellas, I don't know nothin' about nothin'. Man, I'm sorry, I thought maybe you guys wanted to know . . . I mean, I didn't—" He laughed awkwardly again. "I was just in here workin' and next thing I know the window was broke and I don't know nothin' about nothin' and that's what I been sayin' all the time."

They looked at him, their stern faces demanding more.

"In fact, I don't even know why you guys are wastin' your time around here 'cause . . . well, to be honest with you—" He stuck his finger in the face of the dark officer, saw the officer's eyes on his finger, sensed the danger, and reached out and grabbed it with the other hand, smiled and began washing his hands in the air. "I always did think that boy was a wrongdoer. I never have trusted him. Honest, Mister, I don't know nothin' about nothin'. Honest. That's it. That's my story. And

I don't give a damn about nobody else's story. That's mine. I'm dead. I don't know nothin'."

The gray-haired officer picked the narrow cigarettes up, slowly. "I'll just keep these for a while."

"Yes, sir," Fred Jenkins said. "You keep 'em. But like I told you, I ain't . . . if it was up to me . . . there ain't no way . . . you know, I don't even know you. I ain't talked to nobody. I don't know nothin'. All I heard was thunder and lightnin' and saw my window broke and people comin' and that's all I know about whatever happened out on that street whatever day it was."

They nodded in unison. "We might see you again," the dark one said as they started out the door.

Mr. Jenkins forced a laugh. "How you gonna see me *again?* You ain't seen me for the first time yet."

The door closed behind them.

"You bastards," Fred Jenkins said. "You goddamn, dirty, rotten white bastards." He watched them get into their car. "You redneck bastards. You rotten . . ."

Wilford had no idea how easy it had been. He was too young to know how advantageous it was to compromise, or how much grown-ups valued their things, or how little security most people had in this life. He was too young to understand why a man had to protect himself. He was too young to feel a kinship as the audience did. He was too young to feel any adult emotion other than hatred. And now he hated the proprietor as much as he did the policemen. "You *lie,*" he said out loud.

His mother took his hand. "Quiet," she said squeezing it.

The audience rumbled with comments about Wilford's aggressiveness.

The Deputy, hard of hearing, had not heard Wilford, but he could hear the commotion from the audience. "All right," he said. "Let's have quiet in here or I'll clear the room."

Mr. Jenkins glanced at Wilford and his eyes begged for forgiveness. Boy, you're just too young to know, he thought. Shit, I ain't gonna ruin my life for you or nobody else.

"So you don't really know anything at all about this case; is that right?" the Deputy asked.

"That's me. I don't know nothin'."

"All right, then. You're excused."

"Can I leave? I got a store I got to work."

"Sure," the Deputy said. "You can leave. I don't know why Counsel brought you down in the first place."

"Just a minute, Mr. Witness. Mr. Coroner, I have a few questions I'd like to ask this witness, if I may."

"For what? He told you he didn't know anything. Didn't you hear him, Counsel? He said he doesn't know anything about anything. He said he didn't know 'nothin' about nothin'.'"

"Yes, sir, Mr. Coroner, but I might be able to refresh his recollection."

"You can't refresh anything, Counsel. He doesn't know anything. You want to make this thing take all day? Well, we don't have all day to sit here listening to people tell us they don't know anything about the case. Go on, Fred. Go on to your store."

Mr. Jenkins started for the door.

"Just a minute, Mr. Witness."

He stopped at the door.

"Mr. Coroner, am I to be denied the right of cross-examining this witness?"

"There's no cross-examination permitted at a coroner's inquest! I've told you that already, Counsel."

"Well, the right of examining the witness, then. Are you going to excuse him without allowing me the courtesy of examining him?"

"That's right! He told you he doesn't know anything. Now maybe you didn't hear him, but I did." He began working the ball-point for the first time today to settle his nerves. Goddamn smart-ass lawyers, he thought. "Now you listen to me, Counsel. I want you to hear this this time. You're here at the courtesy of the coroner's office."

"I realize that, Mr. Coroner—"

"And that's all. You're not here to try your civil case. I told you that last time. I don't want to have to argue with you every five minutes."

"But you're not allowing me the courtesy of examining this witness."

The reporter wrote furiously, his fingers skipping over the keys. He rocked back and forth as if keeping time with the barrage of words that had suddenly blown up in his face as they both talked at the same time. He was concentrating too intently now to be anything but a medium, transposing the words from his ears to his fingers; but once they slowed down and he was afforded the luxury of time to think, he would be furious with them and would curse the lawyer first and the Deputy second for making his work so difficult, for forcing him to work at maximum efficiency, for forcing him to strain and causing the inevitable headache that would surely be with him when the case was finished.

"And I'm not going to allow you to run this hearing. I'm running it and I'm the one who is going to say when a witness is excused." He waved his hand at Mr. Jenkins. "Get out of here. You're excused, Fred. Now go."

Mr. Jenkins stepped out the door.

"Mr. Coroner, I'd like the record to show that I'm voicing my objection to the witness being excused at this time without my having been given the benefit of interrogating him."

"All right. Let the record show anything you want to. Take his objection down. I don't care how many objections you have, only don't try to run this hearing and don't waste my time with a lot of arguments."

"Mr. Coroner," Blackwell said, throwing both hands out to the side in a gesture of frustration tempered with delicacy, "I'm only making my record. You wouldn't want to begrudge me that, would you?"

"No, no. Not me. You go ahead and make any record you want to. Only don't try to tell me how to run this inquest, Counsel, or you might find yourself outside, too."

"I doubt that, Mr. Coroner. I seriously doubt that the Deputy Coroner would try to remove a lawyer from this room for simply trying to protect the rights of his client. But I don't want to argue with you about the authority or lack of authority of the coroner's office, Mr. Coroner. The witness is gone now and I've made my objection for the record, so I guess any further discussion along these lines is really pointless."

Click-click, click-click, click-click, click-click. He was furious. He had a flashing impression of the transcript and how Mr. Blackwell would look so much superior to him. He couldn't lean over too far for the police. He'd have to control his anger. He'd have to make sure he didn't let Blackwell upset him again. It had been a long time since a lawyer had disturbed him so and forced him to discharge a witness as a way out of a possibly uncomfortable situation. Some of the best ones in the city had tried it and had failed. But the young lawyer in front of him now had succeeded almost effortlessly and the case had a long way to go yet and surely would have many more trying moments. He clicked on with the pen and stared at Mr. Blackwell and for one fleeting fraction of an instant a tinge of admiration crept into his heart.

"Are you through talking now, Counsel?" he asked politely.

"For the record, Mr. Coroner, on the specific issue previously raised, I am officially through talking as of this moment."

The audience laughed.

The Deputy smiled and shook his head.

Mr. Blackwell smiled back at him.

"Wouldn't you like to offer another objection at this time?" he said softly.

"No, Mr. Coroner, not at this time. I don't doubt that I'll have others, but they will be at a later date—if there are any."

"All right. Do you mind if I proceed with the hearing I'm here to conduct?"

"Not at all, Mr. Coroner." Blackwell laughed softly. "Please be my guest."

"Thank you very much, Counsel," he said sarcastically. "It's nice of you to allow me to proceed." He looked at the investigating officer and the smile vanished as his face turned to granite. "Who's your next witness, Officer O'Kelly?"

"I guess the next witness, Mr. Coroner, would be the boy, Earl Carter."

"All right. Where is he?" the Deputy said. "Where's this Earl Carter?"

Mr. Carter and Earl stood up.

"Judge, Yo' Hona," Mr. Carter said. "This here's my boy, Earl, and I brought him here today 'cause the police told me to bring him, but, Mr. Judge, ain't no use in him comin'—"

"Will you sit down and shut up?"

"But, Mr. Judge, Judge, Yo' Hona—"

"I said sit down! One more word out of you and I'll have *you* thrown out of here." He snatched his glasses from the tip of his nose. "This is without a doubt the worst case I've had in years—the worst case I've ever had. I don't want any more outbreaks out of anyone. You understand," he said to the audience. "Now come up here, boy."

Earl's father released his hand and nodded his affirmation.

Earl walked to the witness stand and waited, trembling, for the oath to be administered to him.

■

The system is under constant attack by those who would like to see it evolve into something better for all and by those who would like to move into the position of power and control for their own personal gains. The system is constantly flinching and covering up in defense of its actions. The system is almost never aggressive in instituting reforms that would be for the betterment of all because this usually means that they must amputate one of their inefficient arms, that they must discharge some of their fellow politicians who are involved with the criminal element, that they must replace those who steal with honest people who would ultimately turn on the system.

The system is defensive and must protect itself. The system must survive within the confines of a hostile environment. Therefore, it must be strong enough to ward off opposition from its opponents and its critics.

Many years ago in Chicago another system was in power and it became corrupt, but it did not protect itself and the residents of the city rose up as one voice and voted a reform ticket into office. But the people were smarter than the system then, and were involved with life and were concerned about politics.

The present system is smarter than the people. It has a knowledge of history and it is constantly strengthening itself so that it may *never* be voted out. It is now becoming the biggest business in the city, sometimes with two and three generations voting as they are told to protect the patronage job of one of their family. The system murders all strong opposition in one way or another. The system has but two obligations: to remain strong and assure its future existence, and to continue to provide a safe environment for the gangsters that are so much a part of Chicago's heritage.

The system has a theory about justice: favors for friends, prosecution for enemies. Favors for those who have, prosecution for those who have not. Favors for whites, prosecution for blacks.

But there is a rumbling among the black youth and those who have not. There is an awakening among the youth that says destroy—destroy all old, obsolete systems. There is a vitality that is blossoming among the stone and steel weeds of Chicago. There is, among the young, among the undeformed, the uncorrupted, the uncompromised, a desire to change the way of life. The young, too, like the system, have an awareness of history, and they don't like the history they know. The young are not afraid of losing their jobs. They look forward to the strength it brings to one. The young are not old enough to be silenced easily and the system will have to resort to harsh measures to contain them. And each cruelty that befalls the ambitious young will strengthen them and reinforce their dreams and they will survive and they will fight and they will destroy the system. Then there will be a new system. Then there will be a new city and perhaps . . .

■

"All right, son, before I swear you in, do you go to school?"

Earl stuck his tongue between his teeth and bit down on it until it sent sharp pains darting through his mouth up to his head. Both legs were trembling now and he felt weak, as if he were going to collapse. He held on to the chair; he wet his lips and tried to speak, but he couldn't. He wet his lips again, opened his mouth, and exhaled, but nothing came out except the sound of the air. He couldn't speak. He couldn't even answer yes, and the fear that caused his whole body to tremble now increased and he turned pale and began having difficulty breathing.

"Well, do you or don't you go to school, and do you know the difference between telling the truth and telling a lie?"

He wanted to answer. He tried it again, but all that came out this time was, "I . . . I . . . I . . ."

Wilford slapped his thigh. "Ah, Earl, c'mon, man," he said quietly. "Don't be afraid of that cat. He can't hurt you none."

Earl lowered his eyes, then his head, and stared shamefully at his shoes, worn but polished. He had seen adults in his neighborhood react this way to white people, hiding behind their shell, their protective covering of black ignorance, hiding behind the stereotype that white people understand. And now he was doing it. He was doing it without wanting to. He was afraid of the gray-haired, wrinkled-faced white man who growled at everyone. He was afraid that he might start talking and say something that his father did not want him to say. He was afraid that they might put him in jail, or that his father might lose his job.

That's what his father told him would happen to him if he testified. "You just don't tell 'em nothin', you hear?" his father had said. "White folks leave us alone if we don't bother 'em, and I ain't 'bout to lose my job over somebody who's already dead. You hear? So don't tell 'em nothin'. You hear? You don't know nothin' 'bout nothin'. If they ask you, you don't know. You wasn't in no store and you didn't see nothin'."

He had told Wilford he would not be able to testify. He told him his father would beat him if he said anything about it. He wanted to say something, though, so Wilford would be proud of him. He wanted to talk, but he dared not go against his father. And now, even to say yes to a harmless question was impossible.

The Deputy sighed heavily through his ancient, hairy nostrils. "Well, I'll be. If this don't take all. Can't you talk, boy?" he shouted. Earl nodded his head.

"Well, that's something. Now answer me."

Earl's eyes flooded with tears as he began whimpering softly. The tears overflowed and worked their way down his fat cheeks.

"Just a minute, Mr. Coroner," Blackwell said. "You're frightening the boy. Maybe if you didn't shout at him he might answer some of your questions."

"I've been conducting inquests long enough to know how to talk to children. I don't need any advice from you, Counsel."

"Well, look at him! He's scared to death."

Click-click, click-click. "No one has any need to be frightened of anything at one of my inquests. If he's going to tell the truth, all he has to do is tell it. If he's going to tell us a pack of lies, then he *has* got something to be afraid of. I don't tolerate liars in my room." He looked at Earl. "Are you going to answer me or aren't you?" he asked angrily.

And Wilford thought: Ah, Earl, don't be no chicken, man. I know your ole man—I wouldn't have him for mine—I know he told you not to say nothin', but you could at least lie like a man. You don't have to be no baby, man. C'mon, Earl. C'mon. Try it. Say something to that ole fat cat.

His father stood up again. "Judge, Yo' Hona, when he was a real little boy and he got scared, the same thing used to happen all the time and sometimes he couldn't say nothin' all day. You won't be able to get him to talk now. He's too scared."

"I thought I told you to sit down and shut up!"

"But Yo' Hona, that's my son and I done already told you he don't know nothin' and ain't no need in askin' him 'cause he ain't gonna say nothin' to you now. He don't know nothin'. I told the police that and he told 'em, too. He don't know nothin' 'bout nothin'."

"Well, why didn't you say so," the Deputy said harshly. "Officer, did you get a statement from this boy?"

"No, sir."

"Did you try? Did you interrogate him at all?"

"Sure did, Mr. Coroner."

"What did he say to you?"

"Nothin'. He didn't say one single word to me either."

"I'm not surprised," Mr. Blackwell said. "You probably tried to shake his brains loose."

"Mr. Coroner," O'Kelly said. "Counsel is insinuating something again. He's insulting me and the whole Chicago police force when he does that. Would you tell him to stop saying things like that?"

"All right. All right. I'm sick of these arguments. Both of you stop it. And, Counsel, I don't know where you found these witnesses. This is the second one who doesn't know a thing about the case. All you've succeeded in doing today is wasting my time."

"I don't know how these witnesses were intimidated, Mr. Coroner, but they were. Both the previous witness and this witness were in the store at the time of the incident and if they had been allowed to testify freely they would have told you that the decedent, too, was there. It's the same old story, Mr. Coroner—the police cover-up. They're trying to smear my client's name and prove that he was a criminal when they know it's not true. We know, Mr. Coroner, that this shooting was not done maliciously. In fact, we're inclined to believe that it was an accident as a result of mistaken identity, but the police force won't have it that way. I don't know why they're afraid of the truth. Their officers aren't being charged with anything, and we don't want them charged. All we're asking for is a fair hearing and it looks like we're not going to get one. I've seen some pretty bad things in my day, but I've never seen the authorities stoop this low. Mr. Coroner, when you start intimidating ten-year-old boys you've got a really sick society. If you teach him to lie like this at ten, how can you expect him to be anything short of a murderer when he's seventeen?"

The Deputy was at a loss for words. He played with his pen and strained his mind.

Mr. Blackwell scribbled over Earl's name on his pad. Ah, the hell with it, he thought. "Earl," he said harshly, "you saw them kill Cornbread, didn't you?"

Earl began breathing heavily. His face was streaked with tears.

"Mr. Coroner, it's not worth it to me. I don't want to hurt this kid any more than he's already been hurt. Would you entertain a motion by me to excuse him?"

And then Earl broke down completely, buried his face in his hands, and sobbed.

Poor Earl, Wilford thought, and tears began forming in his

own eyes. He sniffed and wiped his eyes. That's all right, Earl, he thought. You still my buddy, man. I cried the same way when that ole caseworker came by and told Mama that she wasn't gonna get no mo' money from the county. And he wanted to tell Earl that sometimes at night, when he was alone in the house and his mother had been gone for what seemed like hours, he used to start thinking that she would not come back, and he thought it with such convincing intensity that he forced himself to believe that she had been run over by a car or stabbed, or else she was lying in an alley someplace dead and he would be alone—he would even be without a mother—and sometimes he cried until he cried himself to sleep.

"All right, son," the Deputy said gently. "That's all. You won't have to testify. Go sit back by your father."

Earl returned to his seat.

Wilford took his hand and squeezed it. He leaned close to Earl. "That's all right, man," he whispered. "It ain't your fault. I know your ole man wouldn't let you talk."

"Uh huh," Earl said between sobs.

"That's all right. You still my blood brother." Then he searched his mind for something to say that would help his friend, something that would relieve him. "You just a little guy now, but you ain't gonna be little always. Me and you, Earl. When we grow up, me and you—we'll get even with 'em. I promise. We'll get even with 'em. We ain't gonna be scared always, Earl."

Earl kept crying.

"Know somethin'?"

"Uh uh."

"I'm scared, too."

Earl snapped his head up and looked at Wilford in amazement. He cleared his nose. "You?"

Wilford nodded. And then he realized just how frightened he really was.

The Deputy reorganized his papers. He glanced over the statistical sheet and saw that he had not filled in the space reserved for the jury's findings. This was something he usually did shortly after the inquest had begun and he had decided what the verdict should be. In this case he could have done it before the inquest began. There was only one verdict possible. Phone calls from two police captains, one ward committeeman and a man from the mayor's office ruled out the possibility of any other verdict but one. Goddamn, he thought, sometimes it might be nice to call one of these hot ones as I see it instead of the way they want it. And if anything comes of it, if anything happens later on, who catches hell? Me. But there's no heat here. These poor bastards. There ain't one reason in the world why this verdict can't be an accident. That's what it should be. The concern he was showing for the people surprised him. He was getting old, he told himself. He was getting soft. He was allowing himself to be touched. But then he thought he must really be slipping; he must be out of his mind to let a bunch of Negroes upset him so. To hell with the black bastards, he told himself. They got a good lawyer. He'll get 'em something in the civil case. And then he printed in bold letters in the place reserved for the verdict: JUSTIFIABLE HOMICIDE. He pushed his glasses back up, covering the sheet with another piece of paper in case the lawyer happened to come to his desk and see it before he had time to scoop them up and take them with him into the jury room, where he would dictate the verdict to the court reporter, who would type it as he dictated.

"Okay, now, Officer, who's your next witness?"

"That's the other boy, Wilford Robinson."

"Is that the one who gave you a statement?"

"Yes, sir."

Mr. Blackwell interrupted. "The statement he conveniently left behind, Mr. Coroner."

The Deputy ignored him. "All right. Have him step forward."

"Son," his mother whispered to him.

"Yes, ma'am."

"We ain't got nothin' left but us. You wanted to do what was right and I want you to, so you be a man, son. You be a man right here and now and no matter what happens from here on you'll be a man the rest of your natural life."

"Wilford Robinson," the officer's deep voice bellowed out.

The audience became restless. Their uncertainty about Wilford's testimony disturbed them. "They got to him, too," someone whispered. An elderly gentleman nodded his head. "I know," he said, sadly. "They always do."

Wilford nodded to his mother and she sensed his fear and felt the pain again. He had been ten years of happiness to her, and he had also been ten years of pain as she watched him approach adolescence and wondered how long it would be before he was herded off to jail the way his father had been, to serve a life sentence for murder and rape all because he had been standing on the corner talking to the offenders. He hadn't even known of the crime, but he was one of the boys on the street. At that time, at eighteen, he had a record that dated back five years and there was nothing anyone could do to free him. At first the three offenders had sworn that he was innocent, but they could not hold out under the pressure. And the pressure was great. They had robbed a white woman. Then one of the boys had returned to the scene and raped and murdered her. And when they were apprehended, Wilford's father was in their company and was therefore guilty.

He had served nine years of his term and she had given up hope, long ago, of ever seeing him again. But now she had begun to have hope as she watched her son walk to the witness stand. A long time ago—four, five years ago—someone had told her that a good lawyer might be able to get him out. Now she had met the good lawyer and although she didn't want Wilford to know who his father was, she began to think there might be a chance. Things were changing, ever so slowly, but still, they *were* changing. There just might be a chance. And maybe the boy was now old enough to be told the truth. She smiled as she watched him raise his right hand and take the oath. Look at him, she thought. All of a sudden he's gettin' to be just like his father was. Oh Lawd, please don't let 'em hurt my boy.

"You go to school, don't you, boy?"

"Yes, sir," Wilford answered cheerfully.

"And you know the difference between the truth and a lie, don't you?"

He nodded his head.

Mr. Blackwell said, "You have to answer audibly, Wilford. The reporter can't write your answers down if he doesn't hear you."

"Oh," Wilford said. "I'm sorry. Yes, sir, I know the difference."

At this point the Deputy swore Wilford in, and asked his name and address. After he had finished writing them on the witness sheet, he looked at Wilford coldly and said, "What grade are you in?"

"I just started sixth grade. Just this month."

"What happens to little boys who tell lies, son; do you know?"

"Well, first you get a whippin' and then you might go to the devil, too, and all kinds of bad things happen after that, I guess."

Mr. Blackwell smiled.

"I guess you know," the Deputy said. "Did you know this boy, this Nathaniel Hamilton?"

"Yes, sir, I knew Cornbread all my life. Ever since I was a

real little guy. He was my friend. He was all of us friend. He was gonna teach us how to play basketball as good as him and all kinds of things and he was a—"

"All right. All right. Now just answer the questions I ask you. Will you do that now?" The Deputy's gentleness startled Wilford.

"Yes, sir."

"Now on the date and time in question, did you by any chance happen to see this occurrence?"

Wilford began tapping his thigh under the table. "Yes, sir."

"Where were you?"

"In the store."

"What store."

"Mr. Fred's store."

Well, the Deputy thought, here it comes. But what's the difference? After all, what can a ten-year-old kid say to change things? Might as well just let it go as it comes. "All right, now, Wilford, you go ahead, in your own words, and tell me and the members of this jury here and Counsel here everything that you know about this occurrence. Now start at the beginning and take your time and tell us everything that you know."

"Well, first of all, me and Earl—well, no, not me and Earl— it was just me at first. I emptied the garbage and it was just rainin' somethin' awful—and I guess that's why I found them bottles 'cause hadn't nobody else been out there in the alley 'cause it was rainin' so hard. So, anyway, I found some bottles —two of 'em—and I took off over to get Earl. Me and Earl's good friends—always have been. And so, then we left outta his house—me and Earl—and we ran as fast as we could to Mr. Fred's store, 'cause we had them bottles, and for two bottles we could get . . . well, heck, we could get a lotta candy for four cents. And it was still rainin' just as hard—and it never did stop rainin', not for a whole day and night—and we made it to the store. And we was in the store and Mr. Fred had gave me my deposit money and me and Earl was lookin' at the candy trying to figure out what we wanted to get. You know how it is. And next thing we know, in comes Cornbread. And Cornbread, he got two pops and he drank one of 'em and was takin' the other one out and he said to me"—Wilford wiped at the tears that filled his eyes again—"that if me and Earl went by his house after we got what we was gonna buy, that he would give us his bottle, too. And that woulda been two cents more and we coulda bought a whole lot of candy then. And so, anyway, Cornbread left outta the store and we went to the door and watched him 'cause he could run track, too, and you shoulda seen how he ran. He could *sure* run. When Cornbread ran, it looked like he wasn't hardly movin', but, *boy,* he sure was movin'. Wow! Could he run fast." He took a deep breath and shuddered slightly as if he had already relived the part that was about to follow. He glanced quickly at Earl.

Earl smiled and nodded his head encouragingly.

Okay, Earl, he thought. I'm gonna tell 'em for both you and me and for Cornbread, too.

"So then, it was rainin' and lightnin' and thunderin' and Cornbread was runnin' down the block and then this police car pulls up and those guys there"—he pointed to Officers Golich and Atkins seated behind him—"they jumps outta their car and commence to shootin'—just shootin'—shootin' Cornbread! And they wouldn't stop shootin'. They just kept on until he was dead." He took a handkerchief from his pocket, blew his nose, and suddenly he was through crying. He would never have to cry for Cornbread again. He had avenged him. He looked at the Deputy and he said softly, "They killed Cornbread and he wasn't doin' nothin'. All he was doin' was . . . he was just goin' home. That's all he was doin', just runnin' home."

And then he fell silent and the audience was silent, too. A baby began crying and its mother rocked it gently to quiet it, and they all sat still, motionless and silent.

The Deputy cleared his throat and clicked off a thought. "Now you know you're under oath, son?"

"Yes, sir. I told you the truth."

I know you did, son, he thought. But he said, "So that's the way you saw it, anyway. But how do you account for the testimony of Mr. Jenkins? He said the deceased wasn't in his store."

"You mean Cornbread?"

"Yes, Cornbread, the deceased."

"He was in the store, Mister Judge. I know he was in there 'cause I was, too. Earl saw him, too, but can't tell you 'cause— well, 'cause he just can't say it. If he could, he'd tell you I'm right. And me and Mr. Fred, why, we talked about it and he said he was gonna say it, too, but, I don't know—"

"Well, if you say he was there, and they say he wasn't, who do you think we should believe, son?"

"Now, Mr. Coroner, I'm going to have to object to this line of questioning. You yourself said there's no cross-examination permitted at a coroner's inquest and yet you're cross-examining this witness."

"I don't need you to tell me when I'm cross-examining a witness," he said. "Now somebody's lying here." That was always a good tactic. Get two conflicting stories and accuse both of them of lying and then pick the one you wanted. "I don't know which one is lying, but that's up to the jury to decide and I'm sure they will. All right. That's all. Do you have any questions, Jurors?"

And they answered, "No questions."

"All right. Counsel, any questions?"

"No. I have no questions—oh, yes, sir, I do have one."

"I thought you would."

"Wilford," Mr. Blackwell said, "do you know anything about Cornbread belonging to a gang?"

"Cornbread?"

"Yes, son. Did he belong to a gang?"

"No, sir. Cornbread knew everybody, just everybody, but he didn't belong to no gang. Uh uh, he didn't belong to no gang *nowhere*. He didn't have to belong to no gang. He knew everybody and wouldn't nobody—not nobody—bother Cornbread." He smiled. "Not if they knew what was good for 'em they wouldn't bother him. And besides, he was always in the playground playin' basketball or baseball or somethin'. And you know, I remember sometimes at night when you couldn't even see the basket, you'd look over at the playground and there was Cornbread, just shootin' baskets—in the dark! And sometimes when it was quiet—you know how it gets sometimes at night when ain't nobody sayin' nothin' outside—and I could hear that basketball just bammin' and bammin' against the backboard, and I knew it was Cornbread 'cause wouldn't nobody else be out there that late at night. And sometimes that backboard would—bam, bam, bam—would just put me right to sleep. No, *sir*, he didn't belong to no gangs—not Cornbread."

"No further questions," Mr. Blackwell said. "Thank you very much, Wilford. It took a lot of courage for you to come here this afternoon, and I'm proud of you. Thank you, son."

"All right, son," the Deputy said. "That's all. You go back with your mother."

Mrs. Robinson whispered, "Thank you so much, dear Lawd."

It was almost over. The Deputy had rushed through four witnesses without too much opposition. What opposition could there be? The police had done their job well, as usual, and, with the exception of Wilford, there was no evidence to contradict the testimony the investigating officer had presented and that the two patrolmen were about to present. The Deputy felt the record could have been a little less cluttered with arguments between him and Counsel, but he had done what he had to do, and all in all he was satisfied with the way things had gone. It had been a long day—five cases, and he was a little more tired than usual. The burden of protecting his fellow officials was becoming too much for him. He had labored before the public many years and longed for a soft office job where he could sit tucked away in a small room and never have to meet the public. That would be nice, he had often told himself. And come and go as I want to and never have to see anybody except other politicians. That would indeed be a good job. He would do it someday. Someday a member of his ward organization with more seniority than he had would die or retire, and then he would be able to move up into a really good-paying job, maybe even one where he only had to check into the office two or three days a week. But, thinking about it now, he realized that there wasn't anyone in the organization with more seniority than him and that the really good jobs were going to the younger men, the lawyers who already had law practices. But he still hoped that perhaps next year he would get a different position.

Now he searched his mind for a way of shortening the inquest even more. In the past, when there were two policemen involved, he had always called to the stand the one that he felt would make the best witness, and then, rather than call the partner forward to testify, he would simply say, "Officer, your testimony would be the same as your partner's, wouldn't it?" And, of course, the answer was always yes. He filled in the last few lines of the death certificate and tried to decide which of the two officers he would call to the stand.

Both John Golich and Larry Atkins had been moved by Wilford's testimony. They had exchanged glances often while the little boy told his story, and each was wondering how the other felt about things now.

John had not visited the Negro neighborhood again since the day he wandered among them and felt so much compassion for them. He had wanted to return again and feel the vitality that was there. He had wanted to stop at the bars and watch the girls dance. He had even thought of taking his oldest son with him to see and perhaps meet and play with the little sun-baked boys who played their baseball in the street and were so tough that they could slide into an asphalt home plate and never complain of their bruises. And, when he allowed his mind to roam freely, he dwelled on the possibility of his someday stopping into one of the hotels in the area and coming out a new man. He wanted to help these people because now he felt that he belonged to them.

And now he sat in the inquest room fingering his copy of the joint report he and Larry had prepared for their superiors. Basically, it was an honest representation of the facts as they saw them at the time of the shooting. But as he told Larry, there really was no proof that Cornbread was the right man. Perhaps it *was* an accident. Perhaps the man they were chasing did get away. But it didn't really matter because their report was filed with their commanding officer and with the superintendent of police and in a dozen other places; and that report, together with the report of the investigating officer, was the official record of the police department. There was nothing he could do other than take the witness stand and read his report verbatim and stick to it no matter how much pressure the lawyer tried to bring to bear. His guilt was deeply felt, but he had suffered enough, he thought; he had lost many nights' sleep and when he returned to work again he would make it up to the residents of the area in some way. But he would not risk the loss of his job by admitting anything on the witness stand that was not in his report. So long as he testified within the limits of the instructions of his sergeant and lieutenant, he would have the entire might of the City of Chicago behind him and there would be no danger of his losing his job; but if he deviated, if he said one thing that was different from what he was authorized to say, there would be a suspension, and an investigation would follow the suspension and perhaps he would be discharged as a result of that investigation. There was a possibility, however, that he could deviate and still remain on the job, but he would be transferred to a district so far away from his home that it would take him an hour to get there, and once there he would always be assigned the worst jobs. They would harass him until he could take no more and resigned. He hadn't been on the force long, but he had seen this treatment handed out to other officers and they almost never lasted longer than six months. The really strong ones sometimes held out for as long as a year, but they all eventually resigned. No one was strong enough to take the dirtiest jobs in the district and be hounded daily by his superiors and remain on the job. No one could win against the brass.

Larry Atkins had yet to experience guilt. He had finally been released from the hospital, and once he was home his life went on pretty much as it had before the incident. His anger and contempt for his people had increased, however, and when his friends asked him about the shooting he would launch into long tirades about the improbability of anyone from his old neighborhood ever amounting to anything other than a dope peddler or policy runner or pimp or murderer. As far as he was concerned there would never be a truthful word spoken by these people. They were useless, he felt, and would not be missed if they were suddenly erased from the city.

Beatrice despised them for what they had done to Larry, but she could not bring herself to hate them. She had always wanted to be away from them, to be free of them, to be somewhere else and become someone different, but now she was closer to them than ever. She understood why her husband was the one who had to be sacrificed, and although it had given her a great deal of pain, she knew that they had beaten him because they could contain themselves no longer and had to strike out at the authorities. It was sad that Larry was there at that time, and even sadder that he had taken part in a killing of a child, but it was fate, she felt, and there was nothing either of them could do about that. Perhaps it all had a meaning, she told herself, perhaps something really great would result from it. God had always worked strangely, she thought, and she believed this was His work again, but she didn't know where her husband fitted into God's plans or where John fitted in or where the dead athlete belonged in the drama, and surely she didn't know where she belonged. She knew one thing, though: that she could not interfere with Larry's reasoning. Not this time. She could only sit back and watch him destroy himself with hate. She had begun to fall into fits of depression, something that hadn't happened to her since they moved from the old neighborhood, but she hid them well so that Larry never knew that his hatred was also destroying her.

She had also begun to pray with regularity—another thing she had not done in years. Once she thought she might play her game with Larry and in so doing bring the conversation around to the tragedy, hoping to get him to see what he was doing to himself and to admit that he felt some guilt; but Larry had had three Martinis that day, and before she could even start working on him he was shouting to her about how worthless middle-class Negro women were and how fouled up American women were. He was hurting her more every time they argued and she had reached a point where she felt she could not take much more.

And now Larry sat against the wall eyeing Wilford suspiciously. I'll be damned, he thought. I'll be damned. Either that kid's the greatest liar I've ever seen or else he's telling the truth. And if he's telling the truth—goddamn, if he's telling the truth —Oh, Jesus, if he's telling the truth . . .

The Deputy looked at the patrolmen. Well, let's see, he thought. It's a colored case and if I get the white guy the lawyer'll blow his goddamn top, so I better get the colored one, and that way it'll look better. He ran the thought over in his mind again. Yeah, he said to himself, that's the best way to do it.

"Patrolman Golich and Patrolman Atkins, you were both involved in this occurrence, weren't you?"

"Yes, sir," they answered.

"You're partners, aren't you?"

They nodded their affirmation.

"And as I understand it, you both fired at the deceased; is that right?"

"Yes, sir," they replied.

"Okay. Then in that case I'll have one of you take the stand

and the other one will agree with his testimony. Officer Atkins, let's have you up here."

Larry took the witness stand.

"And your testimony, Officer Golich, will be the same as your partner's, won't it?"

"Exactly, sir. We filled out a joint report and everything that's in that report we both agreed to."

"And that report was filed with your superior officer, is that right?"

"Yes, sir," Golich said.

And Larry thought. He really was out of our sight for a couple of minutes. It's possible. It could have happened. He stared at Wilford, trying desperately to find some semblance of the hippies on the block, some slight flaw that would tell him that Wilford was no better than the rest of the scum. He kept staring at him hoping that Wilford would lower his eyes and in so doing confess his guilt, but Wilford never turned away. He looked back at Larry and his lips turned up in a slight smile. He didn't hate the officer any more. It didn't matter what happened now because he had done what he was supposed to do. He had told the truth and even if the officer lied, he knew he had done everything that he could.

I'll be damned, Larry thought. I'll be damned. That little bastard's telling the truth. Ain't that a bitch, he said to himself angrily, he's telling the truth!

"All right, Officer," the Deputy said. "It's late and I don't want to waste any more time here. I've got your name down already." He looked at the reporter. "For the record, Mr. Reporter, the officer's name is Larry Atkins and he's attached to the Eighth District." He faced Officer Atkins again. "Now to expedite things here—because Counsel is probably going to want to ask you a hundred questions—you heard the testimony of the investigating officer, didn't you?"

"Yes, sir."

"All right. And do you concur with that testimony as presented here today by the investigating officer?"

"Well, sir . . ." He paused, looked at Earl, and thought: That poor kid. His father's got no guts at all. And already the kid's finished. A bright kid like that and we had to crush him to make our lie a truth. Then he looked at Wilford, his face streaked from the tears, his eyes fixed in return on him; he looked at the warm, innocent eyes of a boy who would go on speaking the truth and as a result would be at war with the world for the rest of his life. He thought: He's a brave little black bastard. The only goddamn man in the whole place. And I'm supposed to give up everything to save one little black boy who might end up a goddamn bum anyway.

Wilford smiled at the officer as if to say: I understand. I'm too young to know any better. You better take care of yourself like everybody else. It's all right' with me. I understand.

And I'm the one to drive the final nail into his little round, brown head, Larry thought. Look at him, ten years old and already he's been exposed to more of this rotten world than most white kids are at twenty; already he knows all the evils and supreme corruption and decadence of a dying way of life.

"Well?" the Deputy said harshly. "Well, what?"

He ignored the Deputy. Yeah, he thought, me, all by myself, because the system can't be wrong, me chosen as the last word in rubber-stamping a way of life. Black man against black man to maintain a goddamn white lie.

"Larry," his partner whispered from behind him.

Larry turned around and looked into John's frightened face. It's your white lie, he thought.

The audience became restless. "That's a rotten bastard," a man said. "Why don't he go ahead and get it over with like the rest of 'em did? No, he's gotta be cute, he's gotta grandstand and show how important he is."

Larry bit into his bottom lip as he used to do when he was a child and found the pressure unbearable. He hadn't bitten his lip in years. And now he realized that he hadn't really been alive for years, since he stopped fighting the lies made truth. *Somebody's* gotta stop it *somewhere*, he thought. "No." It was out before he could stop it, almost a whisper. A smile crept slowly over his face and he felt warm and alive. He leaned back in the chair and spoke louder. "No, Mr. Coroner. After listening to the testimony of this little boy, I'm not certain this was the man we were pursuing."

The jubilation of the audience drowned out his last three words. They couldn't believe it. They just couldn't believe something was finally beginning to happen.

The Deputy pounded his desk with his open palm. "All right! All right! Let's have some order here or I'll clear the room."

Mr. Blackwell sighed, relieved, but saddened by the birth and destruction of a man.

"What do you mean?" the Deputy asked angrily.

"I mean, Mr. Coroner, that I think the only one telling the truth here today is the little boy." And he thought: The brave little man of the world. The little shit's ruined my whole life. "I mean," he said, speaking slowly and deliberately, "that I believe we made an honest mistake—we could possibly have shot the wrong man, but the circumstances were such that it couldn't happen again in a million years."

John Golich shook his head and thought: You damn fool. You poor damn fool.

"It's hard for me to believe, now, Mr. Coroner, that one of the best boys this neighborhood ever produced could go wrong —not that wrong. We can't prove it, Mr. Coroner, but maybe the guy we were chasing ducked through a gangway or something just before the decedent came out of the store . . ."

Wilford wiped the tears of joy away from his face with the back of his hands. And he began constructing another fantasy. That's just the way my ole man woulda done it, he thought. My ole man woulda been just that great! Hot dog, my ole man . . .